2

Tristitia
A Fairy Tale

Amanda Hocking

Seven Fallen Hearts

www.HockingBooks.com

ISBN: 9798827837152

ⅅEDICATION

To Isley Quinzel, Sawyer Marino, and Swayze Daytona – my furry co-authors.

Other Books by Amanda Hocking

Seven Fallen Hearts
Virtue
Tristitia
A Hungry Heart (Short Story)
Superbia (Coming February 14, 2024)

My Blood Approves Saga
My Blood Approves
Fate
Flutter
Wisdom
Swear
Letters to Elise (Prequel Novella)
Little Tree (Short Story)
My Blood Approves: Complete Saga (eBook Bundle)

Trylle Saga
Switched
Torn
Ascend
Frostfire
Ice Kissed
Crystal Kingdom
The King's Games: A Short Story
The Lost City
The Morning Flower
The Ever After

Watersong Saga
Wake
Lullaby
Tidal
Elegy
Forgotten Lyrics: A Short Story

The Hollows
Hollowland
Hollowmen
Hollowland: Redux
Hollowmen: Redux
Hollow Stars
Into the Hollow Dark
Into the Hollow Horde
The Hollows: A Graphic Novel

Valkyrie Duology
Between the Blade and the Heart
From the Earth to the Shadows

Stand Alone Novels
Freeks
Bestow the Darkness

CHAPTER ONE

TRIS WALKED ALONG THE VESPERTINE SEA on her way to the palace. It was the same journey she'd made hundreds of times before on her way to advise King Dolorin, and so many of those days had been nearly identical.

Until seven weeks ago. That's when her Master had been banished from Cormundie. Since the day he'd gone, subtle but inexplicable changes had started. At night, the moon stayed still but the stars spun around like fireflies, and even the weather and the animals had begun to behave differently.

At first glance, everything on her walk seemed as it had always been. The sea stretched on, dark and ceaseless under a blue sky. Ships came into the harbor, and hungry cats chased rodents and the bird-like harpy goblins as they waited for the fish mongers.

But look closer, and she'd see the rats and harpy goblins chasing the cats. The birds overhead were flying backwards. Nothing quite felt the same.

All of the shifts in nature had begun after Valefor's expulsion, and collectively, everyone called these changes the Altering.

As she veered away from the harbor, she encountered the worst difference. Everyone in the kingdom of Desperationis kept to themselves. "Keep your head down and keep your mouth shut" was practically the motto, and Tris had always liked that.

But now the townsfolk had gotten so chatty. To get to the palace, she had to cut through Little Faunton. It was a bustling but small settlement built near the seaport. Most of the construction had been done twenty years ago, when the fauns emigrated down to the kingdom of Desperationis, and they had built their homes from scraps of wood and cloth from shipwrecks along the shore.

Fauns appeared half-human and half-deer, with the legs, hooves, and small antlers of a deer, while the rest of their body was like that of an ordinary human. Their noses were a bit more rounded, their ears larger and pointed, and they tended to be quite good-looking.

Usually, the fauns kept to themselves in Little Faunton, letting Tris pass by without a word to her, but lately, they would talk to her, commenting on the weather or asking about her day.

"I was having a better day seven weeks ago," Tris muttered, which caused the faun to look at her with a befuddled smile, so then Tris clumsily added, "Good day to you."

The palace loomed above the entire capital. It was a behemoth of stone, carved into the rocky southern face of Mount Salcaelum. All of the elegant flourishes – from the archways to the massive guardian statues flanking the entrance – were made of solid rock. Green vines, leafy ferns, and vibrant moss thrived in the warm climate, and they covered the walls. Only glimpses of the stone underneath were visible, and the lush exterior had given it the nickname the Emerald Palace.

When Tris made it to the royal fortress, she found the King in his throne room. It was a long rectangular room, carved into dark stone. The exterior wall opened onto a balcony, with an expansive view of the entire capital city and seaport. Tris could even see her house on the sea from there.

The throne sat on the dais at the opposite end of the long room, and hardly any of the warm sunlight ever reached it. It was cold and dim by the dramatic chair, even with candelabras on either side. There was only the one piece of furniture in the entire room, and a cauldron tucked away in the back corner for when the King needed to commune with Valefor.

The throne itself was so large, even a grown man looked small in it. The high back was made of the thick bones of a sand leviathan, carved into sharp points arching around it. Whoever sat in the throne looked like they were on the precipice of being devoured.

On the dark stone walls were a few tapestries, all of them depicting long ago battles the King's ancestors had won. Tris heard the subtle sound of wings batting against tapestry, and she spotted an oculatu hiding on one, hanging from the fabric upside down like a large bat.

The oculatus were winged goblins half-the size of a housecat, but their bodies consisted of a solitary eye. They had small leather wings on either side, and a flexible mouth underneath, like that of a snail.

The sonneillons had created them with dark magic a long time ago, and the oculatus served them. Watching, spying, and telepathically sending back all that they saw.

Tris made of note of the oculatu but said nothing as she took her spot before the King.

Standing before the throne already was the faun, Sabina. Her role as seneschal to the King meant overseeing the palace's day-to-day functions.

Sabina was punctual and proper to a fault. She wore a fitted gown of pale blue cotton, and the long hem hid her legs and hooves.

Her soft dress was threadbare and patched in places, and definitely dated in style, but it was still quite lovely with an empire waist and lace flourishes. In it, she'd nearly pass as human, though her exceptional beauty was a giveaway.

The real telltale signs were her three distinct features: a smattering of caramel freckles across her nose and cheeks, two tiny velvety nubs of horns, and her ears came to a tall point, like an elven doe.

Sabina's delicate appearance was a sharp contrast to Tris. Tris dressed more like the pirates her roommate Reni worked with than the kingdom nobility that Sabina was attempting to emulate. A long green jacket, simple black trousers, an off-white blouse, and a leather corset belt made up the bulk of Tris's wardrobe.

"— taxes better spent on the infrastructure than foreign honey," Sabina was in the middle of saying when Tris arrived, but King Dolorin held up his hand to silence her, and he fixed his pale eyes on Tris as she approached.

"Ambrosian honey is a necessity for anyone with sense or wealth, and I have both." The King was speaking to Sabina but glowering at Tris. "We will trade with the kingdom of Voracitas, and that is not up for discussion."

"Yes, Sire, of course," Sabina said with an apologetic curtsey.

"The great Tristitia has decided to deign us with her presence," the King said with an annoyed smile. He sat on a throne made of the bones from a sand leviathan his grandfather had slain, and he perched on the carved ivory as if he had ever felled anything larger than a desert hare.

He was not the first King Tris had worked for, and he was not the first King she had disappointed. She had been the consiliarius for his father Dolian, and before that, Dolian's father Dosorian.

"I'm sorry, Your Majesty," Tris said and bowed. "The streets were busy this –"

"As they are every morning." The King interrupted her with a dismissive wave of his hand.

"Things have been chaotic in the kingdom since the Altering," Trist reminded him.

"That is all the more reason you should be here! I am meant to create order of this, and you are to advise me!" Dolorin shouted, and he glared down at her from under the golden crown set atop his thick black hair.

"That is why Valefor posted you here, to aid me in ruling the kingdom as you aided my father before me," he went on. "You are to help me lead the entire continent of Cormundie into glory and power."

Then he cocked an eyebrow at her. "Or is Valefor no longer your Master since he's been... *relocated*?"

"No, of course I still serve Valefor," Tris said. "He is my Master until my dying breath."

Tris glanced over at the oculatu goblin, watching them, and she straightened her spine.

"Good," Dolorin said with a smug smile. "Now back to the matter at hand. The kingdom of Voracitis is refusing our standard trade arrangement for their honey. They're claiming that the bees aren't producing normally, but it doesn't matter. They have some, I want it, and you need to find a way to obtain it for me."

In a normal season, the decadent golden honey harvested in the valleys of Voracitis was expensive.

Even the King didn't indulge in it daily. Now, with the shortage, Tris and Sabina were expected to find a way to procure it for him.

And so they would. Sabina would even do it with a smile, although Tris had long ago refused such indignities.

All at once, Tris smelled brimstone, and she took a deep breath before turning around. Standing in the entrance of the throne room, a sonneillon waited beside a young man with fiery red hair.

The human she didn't know, but the sonneillon she was all too familiar with. Sonneillons were strange creatures, bipedal and slightly humanoid, but completely lacking in humanity. Their skin appeared to be peeling leather in a deep rusty shade of maroon. Like the fauns, they had small horns on their forehead, but unlike the fauns, theirs were bony and sharp protruding angrily from their skulls. Their legs were more human-esque, but sonneillons had cloven hooves of swine.

Worst of all, sonneillons wore very little clothing. Mephis, in fact, wore almost nothing at all, so the full expanse of his putrid body was visible. Across his bony hips, he had the thin strap of a belt and sheath, so he could carry a dagger made of irin bone. Irin-bone daggers were some of the strongest substances in all of Cormundie, and Mephis claimed he needed it for protection.

Unlike the rest of the sonneillons, Mephis had a pair of trivial leathery wings protruding from his back. They were useless, far too small to lift him off the ground at all, but they flapped whenever he was excited.

"Mephis," Tris said, forcing herself to smile at him. "I didn't know you'd be joining us today."

"It is always so good to see you, Mephis, but your usual courtesy is to call before dropping in," the King said.

"Of course," Mephis agreed, but he sounded undeterred as he and his human guest walked toward the King.

Both Tris and Sabina stepped to the side to allow them to pass by, and Sabina cringed away from the wretched sonneillon.

"Where our Master is now does not abide by the laws of Cormundie," Mephis said with a simpering smile. "We have much to do, and no time to waste."

King Dolorin straightened up and gave the sonneillon a chastened smile. "What does Valefor need done?"

"The Ira was killed nearly two months ago," Mephis explained. "Master lost another peccati when the Luxuria betrayed him. Already he is down to six while the virtus numbers only grow.

"Of all the peccati, the Ira is the most powerful," Mephis went on, and Tris noticed the young man beside him, his chest puffing out as the sonneillon boasted of the Ira's strength, and she groaned inwardly.

With Valefor's banishment after Lux joined the virtus, Tris had been hoping that the Ira's absence would be permanent. All of the peccati were replaceable, and all of them had been at various times. Tris had held her position as the Tristitia for decades, but the Iras tended to have much shorter lifespans.

Ira was wrath personified, in the most literal sense. Uncontrollable rage overwhelmed strength and near immortality.

This fresh-faced human – still a teenager, but tall with arms like tree trunks – beamed when Mephis introduced him, "This is the new Ira."

King Dolorin nodded. "It's always good to have an Ira in my court. But I doubt you stopped by to make introductions."

"No, I'd never squander your time like that," Mephis assured him. "The Master usually trains the peccati himself, but as he's otherwise disposed —"

The sonneillon turned to look at Tris, and her heart sank. The last thing she wanted was to be saddled with a volatile baby.

"Tristitia," Mephis said. "The Master wanted you to show him the ropes, so to speak, and he hoped Ira could stay at the palace, helping to keep King Dolorin safe in the unusual times of the Altering."

"Of course," Tris said, because no other answer would be accepted, and she swallowed down her rising bile as Ira gave her a toothy grin.

CHAPTER TWO

LUMINELLE'S PALACE SMELLED OF LILACS, as it always had every time Indy had been there. The rotunda was glowing, and far off woodwinds played an ethereal melody. It was poised to be a serene vow ceremony.

And yet, Indy felt on edge.

He had been the one that Luminelle tasked with getting the Castimonia ready for her vows, but he had never done so on his own, without the preceding virtu there to help guide their progeny through.

On top of that, it had to be a crash course, with only seven weeks to prepare compared to the literal years that the others experienced. Indy couldn't be sure that he'd done enough.

The attendance for the ceremony was kept small: Luminelle, the Castimonia, and a handful of other irins.

And the *Luxuria*.

Lux stood beside her, dressed in pale blue, while the Castimonia recited her vows to Luminelle.

"I swear on my life, my heart, my soul, that I will forever be faithful to my Mistress Luminelle, never causing her harm, never speaking to her in deceit, never betraying or forsaking her," Lily delivered her oath. "Where my Mistress goes, I follow."

Indy stood at the edge of the room, leaning against a marble pillar, and he watched the ritual pensively.

9

"She's doing well," Aeterna whispered, and Indy glanced over to see his friend standing beside him.

Aeterna was an attractive man with dark brown skin and feathered ivory wings growing from his back. He was one of the younger irins in Luminelle's court, although it was impossible to tell by looking at them. All of the irins – and even the virtus – were ageless and stunning.

"Did I say she wasn't?" Indy asked.

Aeterna smiled. "You didn't need to. I can see the worry written all over your face. You worry too much."

"And you not enough," Indy countered, but he relented under his friend's knowing gaze.

"What are your concerns that keep you from enjoying your hard work?" Aeterna asked.

"How can you even ask that?" Indy let his eyes bounce over to Lux – the first and only peccati to enter Luminelle's palace in the history of the world.

"She has a good heart," Aeterna whispered.

"Yes, she's kind, eager, and a quick study," Indy agreed wearily. "But she was not raised as a virtu, and she still goes by her human name, instead of Castimonia."

"Lily only found out who she was weeks ago," the irin reminded him gently.

"That is my point *precisely*," Indy said. "She hasn't had enough time to understand what she is, and already she's set to marry a peccati." He shook his head at the absurdity of it all.

"It is their love – and Lux's unwavering loyalty to her – that brought about Valefor's banishment," Aeterna said. "We are closer to a victory and peace across the kingdoms of Cormundie, so I don't think we should be so quick to dismiss Lily or Lux."

"No, I'd never want to dismiss them." Indy ran his hand through his dark hair. "I suppose I only worry that none of us are prepared. Valefor will not go away quietly."

"No, he will not," Aeterna concurred, and he put his hand on Indy's shoulder. "But I will be by your side in the dark hours that come before the dawn." Then he motioned to the others who watched as Lily and Luminelle exchanged their final vows. "And so will all your friends."

When the ceremony finished, Lily was pulled into conversation and congratulations with other irins. Luminelle broke off from the small crowd, and as she made her way over to Indy, he stood up straight and smoothed out his jacket.

Luminelle smiled at him, and her dark umber skin glowed subtly. In her pristine gown and glittering jewels, she had a truly celestial beauty. She was the oldest and highest-ranking irin he'd ever met, and she was a matriarch in the most literal sense. All the virtus descended directly from her, with him being her great-great-great grandson. She was Mistress of Light to him and the other virtus as Valefor was Master of Darkness to the peccati.

"Aeterna and Industria," she said when she reached them, and they bowed their heads in deference.

"Luminelle," he said with a tight smile. "It was a truly lovely ceremony."

"They always are," Luminelle said. "Although this one is something special. It should be the last."

"You truly believe that?" he asked, trying hard to mask his skepticism as not to disrespect her. "That the war for Cormundie will end?"

11

"The end has already begun," Luminelle said. "Which is why it's important that we all remain vigilant."

"Indy is nothing if not vigilant," Aeterna said.

"He is well-suited for the times ahead," she concurred with a knowing smile. "I need you both to continue your post with the Castimonia. Lily is not yet ready to work on her own, and given her… *situation*, Valefor will seek to exploit her."

"Of course," Aeterna agreed before Indy could protest. "I'll watch the sky, and Indy will watch her back."

"Thank you for being so flexible," Luminelle told Aeterna.

He smiled. "I do my best. But now I should commend Lily." He left Luminelle alone with Indy, joining Lily and Lux out of earshot in the rotunda.

"You have always been my hardest worker, Industria," Luminelle said, and she rested her golden eyes on him. "So I know that you are not displeased with my request because it is too much work."

"No, of course not." He folded his arms across his chest and lowered his gaze. "And I wouldn't say I am displeased."

"How would you say it then?" she asked him gently.

"Concerned," he admitted, then braved looking at her again. "Can you honestly tell me that you are not?"

"I have many concerns about a great many things," she said, and she let her gaze drift over to where Lily and Lux stood, hand-in-hand smiling at one another.

Then Luminelle looked back at Indy. "But that is why I have you, and the other virtus. I cannot be everywhere and do all things, same as you cannot, but if I do my part, and you do yours, it will make all the difference in the world."

"What if it is not enough?" Indy asked softly.

"What if Cormundie falls to Valefor?"

"We can only do what we can, and what will be, will be." She smiled sadly and put a comforting hand on his arm. "You alone are not responsible for the whole of Cormundie. The humans and animals have free will, and they are beyond your control. Do not let fear overwhelm you or weaken your resolve."

"I do not wish to be so afraid," he admitted.

"Fear is not the problem. The world is a volatile place, and fear is a proper reaction to that," Luminelle said. "But you cannot let it paralyze you. I *need* you. There is much work to be done."

"I will be at your service for as long as you will have me," Indy promised.

13

CHAPTER THREE

THE SMALL CRUMBLING HOUSE built on a rock in the sea had been in Reni's family for centuries. Or at least that's what she had told Tris when she began letting her a room years ago.

Reni's great-great grandfather fell in love with a mermaid, and he built this house so he could watch over her always. All of his daughters and granddaughters had to spend the full moon out at sea, and the house has been in the family ever since.

Tris didn't know how much of that was true, beyond the things she had seen with her own eyes: the house still stood on the rock, and Reni transformed into a mermaid as soon as the light of a full moon touched the Vespertine Sea.

None of that really mattered to Tris, though. The thing that made Reni such an appealing roommate was that the rent was cheap, and Reni spent much of her time away. Either in the sea as a mermaid or sailing it, working on one pirate ship or another. That meant Tris often had the place to herself.

The position as consiliarius to King Dolorin paid very little. He had wanted her to live in the palace, the way she had before when she advised his father. After living under Dolian's roof for many years, with very little space between her work and her life, it had begun to feel rather claustrophobic.

So she made the small stipend work, and she enjoyed living with Reni.

The only way to get to the house was by a rickety bridge over a rocky coast and an angry sea, and few dared make the trek. Tris was especially looking forward to the solitude after a long day of "mentoring" the new Ira.

He talked incessantly, and he had somehow gotten the notion in his head that he knew more about their work than she did, even though he'd taken his vows to Valefor less than a week ago.

All Tris wanted to do when she got home was crawl into her lumpy bed and listen to the waves crashing outside. She was nearly all the way across the bridge before she smelled the ginger, garlic, and hot peppers, and then she noticed the lamplight glowing through the windows.

"Reni's home," Tris realized, and she smiled to herself and picked up her pace.

It had been months since her roommate – and one of Tris's only friends – had been home, and so much had happened.

When she hurried into the house, she found Reni in the kitchen, preparing her delicious ginger garlic chili sauce with fish and vegetables. Her long black braid hung down her back, and her leather vest left her tawny arms bare, showing the scars of her work. Every time she came back, she had a new one.

"So the sea spit you back out again?" Tris asked, greeting her friend with a smile.

"She is a harsh mistress," Reni said with a laugh. She stopped cutting the green beans and yellow carrots and came over to hug Tris.

It wasn't something Reni did often, but it was nice.

"I was afraid you wouldn't be here when I got back," Reni said.

16

Tris laughed. "Where would I go?" They had been living together long enough that Reni ought to know that by now.

"Because." Reni let go of her and looked at her with dark sad eyes. "I heard that your Master was banished, and I have seen the Altering around me."

"He is still my Master, and I am still here," Tris said simply. She kicked off her boots and went over to sit on the bay window bench seat.

Reni watched her expectantly. "*And*?"

"And what?"

Reni let out an exasperated sigh. "What does it mean for all of us now that your Master is gone?"

"Oh," Tris said and shrugged.

Reni grabbed a chair from the dining table, and she pulled it over so she could sit across from her.

That's when Tris saw the fear in Reni's eyes, and she realized she wasn't asking out of curiosity.

"Will all the magic leave the world?" Reni asked in a hushed voice, as if she was afraid to say it aloud. "If magic leaves, what happens to shifting mermaids?"

"No, no," Tris hurried to reassure her. "Magic is a part of the world, as much as the air and the sea. I can't imagine why it would leave."

"But things have *changed*," Reni persisted. "The sea has been angry, the winds have been strong, the fish swim backwards, the bats and harpy goblins are awake during the day instead of at night. The list goes on. The world has been altered."

"Valefor can't step anywhere on the lands of Cormundie right now, but he still has power here," Tris said. "He will return and make things right again."

"He means to return?" Reni asked.

"Yes. He still has time to reset things back to as they were, and he can defeat Luminelle and claim Cormundie once and for all."

"Can he do it?" Reni asked. "Do you believe he can get things back to normal?"

"The Altering has happened because Valefor is not allowed to set foot in our realm," Tris explained her understanding of the situation. "This is Cormundie without influence from the Master of Darkness. The only way I know to return things to as they were is to get him back."

That was the truth of the matter. All those years ago when Tris had joined Valefor as a peccati, she had been enlisted as a soldier to help him defeat Luminelle and her overbearing control.

But Tris's heart had never been in the fight. She didn't much care one way or another if Valefor or Luminelle even won.

Nobody deserved the utopia that Luminelle alleged would happen if she was allowed to control everything. Not a single mortal or monster Tris had ever known had earned that, and none of them deserved to have their sovereignty taken from them in exchange.

No, they all earned the same mixed bag of joy and despair, wine and shite. That was the world Tris worked for – the ordinary, unremarkable, utterly safe status quo.

In her times advising Kings along the Western coast of Cormundie, going where Valefor sent her, she had been carefully doing just enough to keep from tipping the balance one way or another. Although she had made grave missteps under the preceding King Dolian, she had tried to learn from them.

In a war between Good and Evil, Tris wanted neither. She just wanted to be left alone to live her life, and she wanted everyone to live theirs. If only she had understood that before Valefor found her, before she gave her life to him. Because no matter what she wanted, she couldn't be a bystander in the war any longer, not when she was in the middle of it.

"You have been gone so long, and you haven't even told me about it," Tris said, changing the subject in hopes of easing her friend's anxiety. "Did you find any treasures?"

Reni snorted. "We find less and less each time we go out, but I got a really nice sword." Her eyes went down to the chest tucked under the window seat, where she stored the weaponry she found in her travels, most of which were deadly and jewel encrusted. "I'll show you it after we eat."

She stood up and went back into the kitchen to finish cooking. Tris offered to lend a hand, but Reni declined because the meal was almost done.

"You can grab a couple plates from the cupboard, though," Reni said.

"Of course." As Tris went to the kitchen, she asked, "You were gone for two months, and your only excitement was a solitary sword?"

"Well, I did meet an absolutely stunning pirate named Lady Rebellatrix." Reni sighed wistfully. "We only spent a week together, but honestly, she made it all worthwhile."

"Now you have to tell me everything," Tris said, and Reni laughed as she started plating the food.

"I will spare no detail," Reni promised. She paused and smiled over at Tris. "It is good to be home."

CHAPTER FOUR

THE TABLE BEFORE THEM WAS OVERFLOWING with ribbons and lace, flowers and pearls. Lily's nursemaid Nancilla must've gotten everything in the entire kingdom of Insontia for Lily to choose from.

"Your nursemaid is very thorough," Indy said, impressed.

"At least you have enough options so your wedding day will be precisely how you imagine it," Wick said, sounding uncharacteristically optimistic.

Indy was Lily's mentor for her virtu training, and Wick was essentially her witchy godmother, so Lily had enlisted both of them to help her and Lux plan one of the most important days of their lives.

Lux stared at the table with his blue eyes wide and his lips pressed into a pensive line. His blond hair fell across his forehead, and Lily couldn't help but smile.

"What?" he asked.

"Is this the first I'm seeing you overwhelmed?" Lily asked.

"Overwhelmed?" He shook his head. "No, I am excited but I am trying not to show it."

"Truly?" she asked in surprise.

Her nursemaid had always told her that a Prince cares not for wedding planning, but Lux's eyes sparkled when he grinned at her.

"Yes, I've planned a thousand parties, but never a wedding." He slid an arm around her waist, holding

21

her close to him. "And even better, it's the day that I will be joined to you forever. How can I not be excited?"

Lily pulled him into a kiss, because she couldn't resist, and why should she? She and Lux were madly in love, her cruel stepmother had vanished, and the life ahead was full of friends and adventures far beyond her wildest dreams.

Her life had become a wonderous fairy tale, and she was determined to get the most out of her happily ever after.

"*Ahem.*" Wick cleared her throat. "You do have many choices to make if you wish for this wedding to actually happen."

Lily detangled herself from Lux, then gave Wick and Indy an apologetic smile.

"When I have many things to decide, it helps to prioritize," Indy said. "The invitations will need to go out soon, so perhaps the choices should start there?"

"We haven't even decided on the guest list yet," Lily said, casting a glare at Indy.

"I thought that your father and Nancilla were working on that?" Wick asked.

"They are," Lily said. "Except for the ones that are left to Lux and me."

"And we have decided," Lux said firmly, and his eyes had gone cold when he looked over at Indy.

"And I think you should reconsider," Indy said.

"And I think you don't have any say," Lux shot back.

Wick glanced between the two men in confusion, and Lily put her hand on Lux's arm to calm him.

"What is going on with this?" Wick waved her finger between them.

"It isn't wise to invite any servants of Valefor into your home," Indy said, and it was the same disagreement they'd been having for days.

Indy was the Industria, the virtu of diligence. In the time since Lily had met him, he'd proven himself to be just that. His clothing was immaculate, pressed and tailored to a precise fit, and he never had a hair out of place. His chestnut beard was always trimmed and neat, and he had the most serious eyes she'd ever seen. Gray and hard as stone.

"They aren't coming to the palace as servants of anyone," Lux argued. "They would be coming as friends."

"They are peccati," Indy said in exasperation.

"So am I!" Lux snapped. "Or I was. And I wasn't some pure evil monster. We can and do often do the right thing. We have free will, same as you."

"You defected from Valefor, from them," Indy said. "They likely think you betrayed them. You're not even certain they are still your friends."

"Most of them never were," Lux allowed. "But some of them helped me when I was turning on Valefor. Gula and Ava did."

"Gluttony and Greed?" Indy asked with an arched eyebrow.

"For what it's worth, I've met both of them," Lily interjected, hoping to placate Indy. "I don't think they are any more dangerous than Lux."

Indy looked away then, and Lily's heart twisted. He *did* think Lux was dangerous, and that was the problem.

"Are you inviting all the peccati?" Wick asked in an apprehensive way that made Lily look at her.

She'd expected that the witch would be on her and Lux's side on the subject of invitations. Indy was

23

skeptical and serious, but Wick had been an outcast who came to trust Lux. When Lily had first met her, Wick had thought all peccati were scum, but much had changed since then.

Lily had hoped that Wick's heart had softened to all of them, not just Lux.

"Not Ira or Invidia," Lux said. "But the rest of them, yes."

Wick fiddled with lace ribbons and didn't look at anyone when she asked, "You think inviting Superbia is wise?"

"I've never had a problem with Su," Lux answered, and Indy scoffed at that.

"What is your issue with Superbia?" Lily asked, ignoring Indy.

"I knew her years ago," Wick said with an exasperated breath. "She always liked having sorceresses in her court, and I was a young witch looking to escape my provincial town. I was sixteen and I only lasted for six months in the kingdom of Auctoritas before…"

Wick trailed off and shook her head. "Superbia could be relentless, and she nearly drained me of my magic. My time with her is how I learned how wicked peccati can truly be."

"Su is imperfect, but she is civil," Lux said. "We don't have the luxury of turning away allies who are willing to sit at our table. Not now, not against Valefor."

He'd been looking at Wick when he spoke, but he turned his blue eyes hopefully to Lily. He wanted her to support him.

"We are inviting the peccati to our wedding, and we will speak no more of it," she decided.

Wick pressed her lips into a thin line. "I would not want to add to your stresses, so I will keep mum."

"Lux, you have a good eye for party planning," Lily said. "Wick knows everything about flowers. Why don't the two of you put a few things together to narrow it down for me? I need to do some training with Indy."

"If that is what you wish," Lux said hesitantly.

"Thank you." She smiled gratefully up at him. "I won't be gone long." Then she turned to go and motioned for Indy to follow.

"Take your time," Wick said with forced cheer. "Lux and I will have the whole event wrapped up by the time you get back."

Lily led Indy down the hall and into the empty ballroom. None of the candles were lit, and the only light came from large windows at the far side of the room.

"What am I doing?" Lily asked and turned to face Indy.

"I followed you here."

"No, I mean, what do I need to do to prove that I'm truly a virtu so you won't feel the need to worry so much about me?" Lily realized that, to get Indy to trust Lux, she first needed to get him to trust in her. Completing their mentorship might be the only way.

"Ah." He gave her a crooked smile. "Well, we need to continue working on your mastery of the wind. You have a good heart, but you need to be stronger to protect yourself."

"I have killed sonneillons before," Lily reminded him. "And that was before I could conjure the wind."

"Think about how powerful you'll be when you do," he said wryly.

He held out his hand, his palm up towards the sky, and Lily could feel the air in the room already stirring around her. A breeze ruffled her hair, and she put her own hand out.

"Concentrate on the wind," Indy directed her. "Focus on drawing it to you."

Lily knew that she should, but something had occurred to her. It made keeping her attention on the air very difficult.

"Lily, *focus*," he said more forcefully when she let her hand drop to her side.

"Have you ever killed anyone before?" she asked.

"What?" The wind suddenly dropped, and Indy narrowed his eyes at her. "Why would you ask that?"

"Because…" She chewed the inside of her cheek and avoided his gaze as she tried to find the words. "Because you're a virtu. You're good, and you're teaching me to harness my powers to protect myself. But… I've killed before, and so has Lux. Are we still good?"

"Just because we are good does not mean that we need to lay down for other's cruelty. In fact, it should mean the opposite," Indy said. "Sometimes, we will have to use violence to protect ourselves and others, and those actions may lead to death."

"And that's okay?" Lily asked. "Luminelle sanctions that?"

"Of course." He tilted his head, and his dark eyes were dubious. "Do you think she expects us to stop Valefor by lying down and dying in front of him?"

"No, I should hope not."

Indy's arms were folded across his chest, and he stared out the ballroom windows at the overcast sky.

"The first time I killed was before I had even taken my vows."

"*Really?*" she asked, surprised.

"I was fifteen, living at home with my family," he explained. "My father was the Industria, and I was apprenticing him. But I still had something of a normal family life. I had time for books, fishing in the stream, and riding horses with my younger sister Irisia.

"Irisia was a few years younger than me, and she…" His jaw tensed for a moment. "She was kind and jubilant, and you remind me a bit of her. She loved horses and fairy tales, and she even kept a field mouse as a pet."

Lily smiled at that. She had a pair of chubby little mice, Polly and Poppy. Before she had met Lux, they had been her only friends. Even now, when her life was much fuller than she'd ever dreamed it could be, she still found so much joy from cuddling with Polly and Poppy or watching them play.

"We had gone out riding one afternoon, through the wildflower fields of the kingdom of Zelus," he said, and his voice had gotten thicker. "We weren't bothering anyone, but an angry centaur came upon us."

Centaurs had a human torso, head, and arms on top of the body of a horse. Lily had never met one before, but in the books she read, the centaurs lived the same as humans, although their houses were more like stables.

"He was enraged that we were riding horses," Indy elaborated. "Most centaurs aren't bothered by it, but some consider it akin to bondage.

"Neither of us wanted any trouble with him," he continued, his words growing harder. "We got off the horses, and Irisia tried to explain how much she loved hers, how much time she spent ensuring they were happy and well cared for."

He shook his head. "The centaur didn't care. He didn't listen. He just reared up and… stomped Irisia like she was a bug. He killed my little sister before I had a chance to do anything."

Indy fell silent then, though the story didn't feel over.

"I couldn't let the centaur go," Indy said at length. "He couldn't just run around killing innocent girls. I didn't have mastery of the wind, not then, but my father had taught me enough to conjure it, and my anger helped with the rest.

"I summoned all I could, and the gust knocked him to the ground," he went on. "Even nearby trees fell down. I grabbed a branch that had broken off, and it was still thick and heavy."

He stared off again, then shook his head and gave her a sad smile. "I will save you the gory details, but the centaur didn't live. I killed him to avenge my sister and to prevent others from suffering her fate."

"I'm so sorry," Lily said.

"It was a very long time ago," he said, but she could see the pain still lingered in his eyes. "My point is that I have killed since then, and so will you. We're at war, Lily, and it's not going to be kind or easy."

He stepped closer to her and put a hand on her shoulder. "I will do all that I can to protect you, but the best way I truly can is by teaching you to protect yourself. Now come, focus and learn to harness the wind."

CHAPTER FIVE

IN HER CHANCERY OFFICE in the Desperationis palace, Tris sat at her desk reading King Dolorin's correspondence, but Ira wasn't making it easy. He skulked around the room, sighing and touching the books on her shelves.

"You can read something, if you'd like," Tris suggested, for the third time. She'd tried to get him to help her read the letters, and when he'd declined, she pointed him to a book on daemonology that Valefor had written.

"I wouldn't like to read anything," he grumbled. "I would like it if you showed me what it means to be a peccati. Valefor told me about the powers and strength that I can access as the Ira, but I hardly know how to use any of it."

"Being a peccati isn't all fun and powers," Tris said. "Most of it is mundane, like reading through the King's mail. I'm doing this because I have to if I mean to advise the King properly. *This* is where Valefor wants me, this is what he's tasked me with doing."

He shook his head. "But that's not what I'll do as the Ira."

"You might," she countered, and his face paled. "Do you think Gula just sits around and eats? Or that the last Ira just ran around punching things?"

He seemed genuinely confused, his brows pinching together as he scowled. "They don't?"

"Some of the time, maybe, but our work cannot be so narrow," she explained. "We run errands for Valefor, and we influence mortals to follow his will. A King has influence over many, many mortals, so when I guide him, it has a much further reach."

"Then I shall influence a general on a battle front," Ira declared, sounding much like a small child who has just decided they want to be a lion tamer or a shimmering knight. "I don't have to stay cooped inside."

He cast a disparaging gaze around the bookshelves. "You probably like this, don't you, *Tristitia?*" He used a sing-song tone for her name, and he smirked at her, like he thought he was so clever. "You are Sloth. The *lazy* one."

She glared up at him. "That is a crude translation. 'Tristitia' means sorrow, despair, the absence of exertion."

"So you're not lazy, you're sad?"

"Such a simplification." She rolled her eyes and leaned back in her chair. "Do you know what the largest predators in Desperationis are?"

He laughed. "No. Why would I?"

"Well, I do. We have the leoles, the crocotta wild dogs, and the sand leviathan. The leoles, as winged lions, sleep twenty hours a day. The crocotta dogs sleep for days at a time, and the sand leviathans are only awake for a matter of weeks out of the *entire* year.

"But they are not lazy," Tris went on. "They are apex predators conserving their energy."

"So you're conserving your energy?" he asked dubiously. "For what?"

"For whatever I need. Like –" Tris waggled her fingers at him and focused on Ira. "– *this.*"

All at once, his eyes rolled to the back of his head, and he crumpled to the floor, unconscious. That was one of the benefits of being the Tristitia – she could put anyone to sleep with her mind.

Tris went back to dealing with the King's correspondence while Ira snored loudly on the rug in the middle of the room. She hadn't made it much farther when Sabina knocked timidly at the door. The faun glanced down at Ira then gave Tris a sheepish smile.

"Sorry, I don't mean to bother you," Sabina said. "I can come back later."

"Now is actually a good time if you want to talk to me without Ira in the way," Tris said and motioned for Sabina to enter.

Tris never minded having her work interrupted, and she rather liked Sabina. The faun was quiet and stayed out of her way for the most part, and Sabina's main concern was keeping the kingdom safe and the people happy.

Sabina carefully stepped around Ira, her hooves padding lightly on the rug, and she sat in the chair across from Tris's desk.

"We need to talk about honey," Sabina said.

Tris groaned. She had nearly forgotten about the King's ridiculous demand for ambrosian honey. "So, how are we going to get him his damned honey?"

"I talked to a Voracitis seneschal, and they said they'd be willing to part with half of their usual order," Sabina said. "We would have to pay for that with twice as many crates of bananas as we usually trade."

Tris leaned back in her chair. "Can we afford that?"

"With the Altered weather behaving so strangely, it's affected the crops." Sabina shook her head sadly. "We had that late frost that wiped out so many fruits and vegetables, and the winds and rains have been too much, washing out gardens and fields.

"My people have been through a famine before," Sabina went on, speaking slowly, and her gentle eyes were on the floor. "I was young when we left Desiderium, but my parents, my neighbors, my friends, they all have told me about what it was like when there wasn't enough food."

The faun lifted her head and looked up at Tris. "I know what we need to do to avoid that, but it involves rationing. We need to stock up our reserves, and then only take from it what we need."

"I don't know how I'll get the King to agree to that." Tris sighed and sunk lower in her chair. "How much food do we have now? How long before starvation is a problem?"

"We do have some time," Sabina replied carefully. "But the sooner we begin storing food, the safer we'll be."

"I know, I know." Tris leaned her head back and stared up at the ceiling. "Give me some time. I have to figure out what to say to the King."

"Thank you, Tris."

CHAPTER SIX

TRIS WORKED LATE INTO THE EVENING, thinking on her conversation with Sabina and trying to come up with a solution. Ira hadn't made that easy, because he'd been grumbling and annoyed since she'd knocked him out.

Sabina offered to take Ira out to a tavern as a way of placating him, and that got him out of Tris's hair so she could plot. To convince King Dolorin not to let half his kingdom starve, Tris needed to find a precedent. If his father or grandfather had done something similar in the past, Dolorin would be more easily swayed.

Unfortunately – but entirely unsurprisingly – Dolorin came from a long line of selfish, paranoid fools who valued suffering. Despite her best efforts, Tris found nothing to support her cause.

It was dark out by the time she made her trek home, trudging through the lively Little Faunton and the quiet boardwalk along the shore. Her house on the rock was all lit up, and the sea air was scented with mangos, ginger, and basil. That was another of the upsides of having her roommate home. Reni was an amazing chef who loved to cook.

But as she reached the door, Tris heard one of the downsides of life with Reni – the sound of a man's laughter coming from inside. Reni had company.

Tris took a fortifying breath, forced a smile, and reminded herself that an amazing meal and her lumpy bed waited for her inside. Then she opened the door.

Reni was in the kitchen. Her long dark hair was pulled up with a scarf around her head as she worked at the stove.

"Tris, you're finally home!" Reni grinned at her. "Your friend is visiting."

"My friend?" Tris asked, and her eyes followed to where Reni pointed.

A man was sitting with his back to her, and his boots were propped up on the table. He was lean, dressed in lush satins and embroidered leathers, and his dark locks were pulled up, so she could see the golden chains around his neck.

It was Avaritia, her peccati brethren.

"Ava, what are you doing here?" she demanded when he faced her.

"Your lovely roommate was keeping me entertained while I waited for you," he said. "She even put me to work peeling mangos and slicing cucumbers."

"I was working late," Tris replied vaguely, and she narrowed her eyes at him, trying to get a read on what he wanted.

He smirked. "I never pegged you for a hard worker, Tris."

"And yet you pegged me as someone who enjoyed an unannounced visit?" she countered.

He lifted his chin slightly, appraising her. Ava was charming, handsome, stylish, and he only visited her when he needed something.

"I should've sent word ahead, but I was in the area and decided to drop in for a friendly visit," Ava assured her, and he rose to his feet. "Come in, come

34

in. This is your home. No sense in hiding by the door."

Tris hadn't moved since she'd stepped inside, but she relented and sat on the bench in the bay window.

"He really hasn't been much of a bother," Reni said cheerily. "But I'm happy to throw him out if you wish."

"And I'd be happy to go." Ava held up his hands, palms out. "Truly. I am here for a chat."

"Did Valefor send you to check up on my progress with Ira?" Tris asked.

"Actually, I haven't spoken much to Valefor since... he's been gone," he said and sat down on the chair nearest to her. "But I had heard about the new Ira. How is he?"

Tris shrugged. "Obnoxious and smug, but still better than the old one."

Ava laughed and settled back in the chair. "Well, I am not jealous that you've been burdened with him."

"If it's not our Master or Ira, what exactly has brought you here?"

"Why, the wedding, of course," he said.

"What wedding?"

His eyebrows arched in wonderment. "*The wedding* between the peccati and the virtu. The union that banished our Master, launched the Altering, and put all of Cormundie in jeopardy."

"Oh, right. I haven't given it much thought," Tris said, and Ava was dumbfounded. "I haven't seen Lux in years. I'm busy with the new Ira and the kingdom of Desperationis."

"That is certainly one way to react," Ava replied.

Tris sighed. "And what is the way that *you* reacted?"

He waited a beat, toying with the many expensive rings on his fingers. He lowered his eyes and licked his lips before quietly asking, "How badly do you want Valefor to return?"

She shook her head, certain she'd misheard him. "*What?*"

"Invidia is quite keen to get Valefor back to his lair here on Cormundie," Ava said. "I've also heard rumors that Superbia and the new Ira are supporting him.

"Luxuria has turned against Valefor," Ava continued. "Gula has sided with Lux." He looked up at Tris.

"And that just leaves the two of us," she finished for him.

"I have found myself much happier without a Master meddling in my affairs and tasking me with tedious errands," Ava said. "Wouldn't you prefer a world where there is no one to burden you with Ira?"

"My preferences rarely matter in the grand scheme of things," Tris replied evasively. "What's done is done, and what will be, will be."

"We're not talking about whether or not the sun will rise tomorrow." Ava leaned forward and rested his arms on his legs. "Valefor has been banished, and some of the peccati are working to keep it that way. I want to help them, and I want you to help us."

"How?" Tris asked.

"We need to shore up the numbers." He reached into his breast pocket and pulled out an embossed, lacy parchment. "I was invited to Lux and Lily's wedding."

"*Lily?*" Tris asked as she tentatively took the paper.

"That's what the Castimonia goes by," Ava said, and she rolled her eyes. "I'm going to the wedding in Insontia, and I want you to go with me. Maybe Su will join if I can persuade her. But then we'll all be able to work together to stop Valefor from returning."

Tris snorted. "You make it sound so easy."

"Maybe it will be," he said, seeming more hopeful than she would've expected from him. "When was the last time there has been a meeting of the peccati? Who knows what will happen if we all work together?"

"Well, not all of us," Tris pointed out. "It will only be five at best."

"Ira and Invidia rarely have anything interesting to say," Ava said with a shrug. "But you could always bring Ira along if you think it would be worthwhile."

"No," Tris said before giving it any thought. "No. I don't trust him."

"Does that mean that you are coming?" he asked, his eyebrows raised brightly.

She sighed and sunk back on the bench seat. "I don't know how I could, even if I wanted to. I'm not like you or some of the others, who can come and go as you please. I work closely with the King, and now I've got Ira to contend with, too. And while yes, I would love a break from all of that, the King isn't going to just let me waltz off to visit the traitorous Luxuria and plot to overthrow Valefor."

"Then lie to him, Tris." Ava gave her a wry smirk. "Certainly you've had plenty of experience with that."

"She's just looking for an excuse," Reni said as she came over to them. "She'd never leave Desperationis if she had her way."

Reni brought three plates over, handing one to Tris and one to Ava, before taking a seat and a plate for herself. All of them were piled high with bright mangos, cucumbers, peppers, and a ginger sauce poured over the pale pink meat of the sea prawns.

"Oh, Reni, this looks amazing." Ava awed over the savory meal. "You are much too generous."

Reni flashed a proud smile. "I cook a lot when I'm at sea with a crew, and I love it because there's so many fresh ingredients we catch at sea or going to different ports."

Ava had taken a mouthful of the food, and immediately moaned with pleasure. Tris was much less exuberant about it than he was, even though she did think it was delicious, but she'd never been as prone to spectacle as him.

"This is fantastic, Reni," Ava said after he'd swallowed his first bite. "Tris might not appreciate what she has here, but I am ready to run off and marry you if it means more of this."

Reni laughed. "As tempting as that offer is, I'd miss the sea too much, and you're a bit too… not a woman for my taste."

"Fair enough," he said with just a hint of disappointment. "But if you ever change your mind, the offer still stands." Then he looked over at Tris. "Is that why you don't like travelling? Nothing ever tastes as good as a homecooked meal?"

"That certainly helps," Tris admitted. "Travelling has just never been that appealing to me. It's dirty and exhausting, and it's usually dangerous."

"But you get to see things you've never seen before," Ava said.

"That might be a better argument if I wasn't going to a stuffy wedding at a palace," Tris countered. "I've been to enough of those, thank you."

"There will be a banquet," Ava said, trying to tantalize her. "I've heard that since Gula is from Voracitas, he's smuggled in some ambrosian honey for the cake."

"I've never been that into sweets," Tris muttered, because honestly she was sick of hearing about the damned honey. The King already expected her to procure some.

"Well, what is it that I can offer to entice you to join me?" Ava asked.

She narrowed her eyes at him. "Why are you so set on me going with you?"

"Because it's as you said." He set his utensils on his plate and looked her in the eyes. "We can't even get all of us together. At best, there will be five of us. But you've always been the one I could count on, much more than any of the others."

In the many years that they'd both been serving Valefor, Ava and Tris had crossed paths more than a few times. He had a bad habit of getting himself into tight spaces he couldn't talk or bribe himself out of, and that's when he had to turn to Tris.

"Tristitia, please," he implored her. For a moment, he let his confidence fall away, and the vulnerable fear in his eyes was enough to stir something inside her. "We can really change things, for once in our ridiculously long lives. Help me set us free."

She chewed the inside of her cheek and stared down at the floor. "I think I know how I can get out of Desperationis long enough for the wedding."

CHAPTER SEVEN

INDY HAD BEEN PUSHING LILY through her training as quickly as possible, and to her credit, Lily was a hard worker.

But her impending nuptials had been encroaching on more and more of her time. It made sense, but Indy still found the whole thing unnerving. Lily hadn't even completed her training yet, and she was rushing off to marry a peccati.

Luminelle had given the union a blessing, so he knew he shouldn't worry.

But still he did.

No matter what Lily, her friends, or her family might say, Indy didn't trust Lux. But oh, how Lily tried to assuage him.

She pulled him aside and all but begged him to go to Lux's stag party.

"It will give you a chance to know him better," she insisted, beseeching him with her dark eyes. "I know you don't like him very much."

Indy couldn't argue with that, so he lowered his eyes and fiddled with the cuffs of his shirt. "I hardly know him at all."

"That is my point precisely," Lily said, and she put a gentle hand on his wrist so he'd stopped fussing. "Go along on the stag party. Have fun. I know you'll come to see the good in him that I see."

Lily reminded Indy so much of his little sister when she looked at him like that, and he'd hardly been able to deny Irisia, either.

So he'd smiled at her and said, "Of course."

That was how Indy ended up in the vast dining hall of the Insontian palace with Lux's pitiful circle of friends – another peccati Gula, his future father-in-law King Adriel, a minstrel faun called Felix, and the irin Aeterna.

A feast of Insontia delicacies had been spread out on the table: boar, snails, river oysters, cheeses of all types, figs and pomegranates, as well as several loaves of different kinds of bread. Lux sat at one end of the table with the King at the other. Because he was here to get to know him better, Indy chose the seat to Lux's left, across from Gula.

While the old friends talked and laughed, Indy picked at his food and watched them. He wanted to eat, but his stomach kept twisting, and he found himself fidgeting more with the figs than consuming them.

"So what type of debauchery usually happens at these parties?" Indy asked.

"The plan tonight is to keep the debauchery to a minimum," Lux said with a smile that Indy couldn't quite read.

"Really?" Indy quirked an eyebrow. "I expected you'd want something bawdier."

"If I wanted something bawdy, I wouldn't have moved to Insontia to marry Lily," Lux said, then he turned to Gula and patted him warmly on the shoulder. "The only decadent thing here is the feast that Gula so graciously provided."

Everyone joined in on praising Gula and the hearty meal, and the conversation moved onto the unusual weather they'd had lately. This time of year should have been warm and pleasant, but it had been rather chill with excessive rainstorms. At least today had been dry.

Indy leaned back in his chair, nibbling at his meal and watching Lux talk and laugh with his guests. He was charming and radiant, and those traits certainly made him likable, but they didn't necessarily mean he was *good*.

Later on in the night, after they'd finished the first few courses of their heavy meal but before the dessert had been brought out, the women came down to join them.

Lily had something of a hen party with Wick and Nancilla, but they wanted to join in the festivities with the men, which included sumptuous desserts, music of Felix playing with his minstrel band, and dancing throughout the room.

When the party was in full swing, with everyone laughing, dancing, and generally being merry, Indy stood at the edge of the room, watching them all with an anxious smile. He alone remained sober when everyone else was drunk on love and happiness.

Lux spun Lily around the dancefloor with great flourish, but he politely allowed her father to cut in. As King Adriel and Lily did a more chastened arm-in-arm dance, Lux grabbed a mug of ale and joined Indy.

"Everyone seems to be having a wonderful time," Indy said.

"Everyone but you," Lux commented, then took a long drink. "You don't trust me. That much I understand."

"I am glad you understand," Indy replied flatly.

"I know better than anyone that Lily is very special," Lux said, and he finally looked over at Indy.

Until then, both men had been staring straight ahead at the revelers. "But what I haven't deciphered is what exactly Lily is to you."

Indy realized that Lux was studying him, and what he'd mistaken for coldness was actually a wary uncertainty.

"Do you feel anything for your brethren?" Indy asked.

"I care for Gula a great deal, and I have fondness for those that have helped me," Lux said. "But no, I don't feel anything more than that."

"Did you have any siblings? Back before you became a peccati?" Indy pressed.

"A much younger brother, but we never got along."

"Maybe that's part of it then," Indy said. "I was close to my sister, and the virtus are of my blood. They are as much my family as any sibling raised alongside me."

"When did you become a virtu?" Lux asked.

"The day I was born, I was already intended for it, and on my twenty-first birthday, I took my vows, and my father died," he said.

"It always seemed to me that you virtus got the short end of the deal," Lux mused. "You never had a choice in any of this."

Indy bristled. "You *chose* this. I've always thought that was much worse."

"I didn't realize what I was agreeing to." Lux sighed. "It's impossible to truly grasp what being a servant to Valefor means."

"So did the choice even matter?" Indy countered. "If we can't truly know what we're becoming?"

Lux considered it a moment before deciding, "I don't know. But it is still nice to be asked."

"Who were you before you were the Luxuria?"

"I was Maxon, heir to the throne in the kingdom of Desiderium," Lux said. "I was spoiled and lonely, and I was a hopeless romantic."

"That's how you ended up working for Valefor?"

"That's the short version." Lux cocked his head and smirked. "Come to think of it, that's also why I left him."

Lux looked out at the dancefloor, his eyes alight as he watched Lily dancing and laughing with her friends. "She is my heart, and I love her beyond anything I ever thought possible."

"I know you do," Indy allowed. "But do you think you're ready for what you're going to face? Your Master's wrath —"

"He is *not* my Master, not any longer," Lux cut him off sharply. "I swore my fealty to Lily, now and forever. She may not yet be my wife, but she is already my Mistress. I serve no one higher than her." His voice trembled with his conviction.

"That's all the more reason for Valefor to be enraged," Indy said. "Call him whatever you like, but his wrath is still something you must contend with."

"Are you asking if I am prepared for the hellfire Valefor will reign down on myself and Lily if he's ever allowed to return to Cormundie?"

"To put it succinctly, yes," Indy said.

Lux leaned in toward Indy and lowered his voice slightly, as if they were conspiring. "In the interest of candor, no. I'm not even remotely prepared, and neither is she. But that's why you're here, isn't it? To keep her safe?"

"I'm here to mentor her because her mother wasn't here to do it," Indy replied evasively.

"But Luminelle chose *you*, Industria, specifically, even though there are another five of you that could mentor her just as well. I don't know that much about virtus, but I've heard that you are the Light's answer to Ira. The one with the brute force."

Indy stiffened. "I'm hardly a brute."

"You are strong. That's why Luminelle chose you to protect Lily from Valefor."

"And from you, if need be," Indy added.

Lux grinned at that. "Good."

CHAPTER EIGHT

TRAVEL TO THE KINGDOM OF INSONTIA had been long and unpleasant, and she arrived the day before the wedding. Carriages couldn't pass through the Morsenea Desert, so Tris had to go the long way on the Great South Road to get here from Desperationis. The trip had taken her several long days, and she was exhausted.

The only way she'd even been able to secure her absence was by telling King Dolorin that she'd get his ambrosian honey. That meant that her trip home would take even longer, because she'd have to venture to southern Voracitas and the Apisius Valley for the damned honey.

At least she had a break in her journey. Or so Tris told herself as she stepped out of the chartered carriage just inside the walls that surrounded the capital city of Insontia. The streets were much too crowded and narrow for the carriage, and she'd have to go on foot the rest of the way, carrying her hefty luggage herself.

She stretched her legs. Her leather pants clung uncomfortably tight to her thighs, and she cursed herself again for her choice in apparel. She journeyed so little because she hated it so, and she hadn't thought enough about travelling attire.

In fact, she had never been to Insontia before. Valefor's work kept her on the west coast. Insontia was much farther inland than her seaport home, and it was a beautiful land of lush green rolling hills.

The palace was at the top of the hill straight up the road from where she stood. She could see the spires touching a sky of summer blue and wispy clouds.

The streets were crowded with guests and revelers. Tris guessed that half of the people of Insontia had been invited, or at least that's how it seemed. Every piece of conversation she overheard was about one aspect of the wedding or another:

Did you hear they're having delphiniums?

The Princess is being wed with a unicorn officiating, I swear that's what the cake maker told me.

Her gown is said to be the same color blue as the bridegroom's eyes. Isn't that so romantic?

"Ridiculous," Tris snorted in response, and hurried on her way when she received a strange look. "Damned Ava."

She never should've let him talk her into attending this travesty. Admittedly, she wanted Valefor to return even less than Ava did, but his plan sounded flimsy. Getting all the peccati working together to overthrow their Master? It was more a flight of fancy than anything else.

But still, Tris had to try. She often daydreamed of a life without a Master, without service to another brat King, to live as she pleased.

So she chased after Ava's plans because it was better than doing nothing at all.

Ava had booked rooms at an inn near to the palace, and she desperately wanted to get there. She needed to change out of her awful pants and wash off the grime from the road, but mostly she wanted to get away from the crowds.

Tris finally made it up the hill, to just outside the palace gates, but she hadn't yet seen any sign of the Fabula Inn. She double checked Ava's instructions – he'd scrawled them in his elegant writing on the back of the wedding invitation – but she was definitely lost.

"This is why I don't travel alone," Tris muttered to herself. "And also why I don't travel."

She had wanted Ava to go with her, since he was so insistent about her attending this debacle, but he had other peccati to visit, so they had to travel separately.

"Are you lost?" a warm voice asked her over her shoulder, and she whirled around to see a pair of gray eyes holding hers.

They were, of course, attached to a man. A handsome young man, Tris realized when she actually got a look at him. His hair was thick and dark, and a beard hugged his sharp jaw.

But for a moment, she'd only been able to see his eyes. They were as hard and silver as any blade, and so strangely captivating, she couldn't breathe for a moment.

She could swear she'd never met him before, and yet, when she looked into his eyes, she recognized something she saw there.

"What?" Tris asked because she'd forgotten his question.

His expression shifted to concern, his eyebrows pinching together slightly and his eyes softening. "Are you lost?"

"I am, actually. I'm here for the wedding, and I can't seem to find the inn I'm booked at."

"I'm not from Insontia, but I've been here long enough to know my way around," he said.

"I'm looking for the Fabula Inn."

He smiled, a broad enchanting thing. His eyes were still so serious, but his smile let a bit of his light escape, like the sun parting storm clouds.

Pointing down the road, he said, "It's just right this way. I can show you."

"Thank you."

He offered to take her bag, and because she was tired from the journey already, she let him. As they walked, his steps fell right beside hers.

"Bride or groom?" he asked.

"Pardon?"

"You said you were here for the wedding. Are you on the bride or groom's side?"

"Which one do you think I am?" she asked.

He cocked his head and studied her a moment. "Are you a friend of Lily's?"

Tris shook her head. "I've never even met Lily."

"So you're a friend of Lux's," he guessed, and his earlier cheer evaporated. He frowned, but his somber eyes still flickered with something familiar.

And then it all clicked for her.

She stopped, so he stopped too. "You're a virtu," she said.

"And you're a peccati," he replied.

She nodded once. They started walking again, though they both eyed each other up warily.

"I gather you're not the Castimonia," she said.

"And you're not Lux or Gula, because I've met both of them," he reasoned.

"You're astute, tall, and severe," Tris said, listing what she knew about him so far.

"*Severe*?"

"Aye. I've met undertakers with more humor in their eyes," Tris said, and she was only exaggerating a little.

"That is a very grave accusation," he said with a wry smirk.

"You're not Pazenezia, because I've heard she's a woman," Tris said. "Moderatio is rumored to be a man, but there's nothing moderate about you, is there? No, you wear your intensity like a cloak."

She chewed her lip as she studied him, narrowing down her options. "You are the Industria."

"Most everyone calls me Indy, but yes, that is my official title," he said, looking somewhat impressed that she'd clocked him so quickly.

"Indy," she repeated. "I wouldn't have predicted you as the nickname type, but I like it."

"So, who are you?"

"Aren't you going to guess?"

"Hmm." He thought about it as they walked. "You're short, clever, and lovely, and you're also tired. Or maybe I just bore you."

"Perhaps it's both?" she teased.

He appraised her again, and she could feel his eyes searching hers. "You are my other side. You're the Tristitia."

"Tris."

"It's nice to meet you, Tris."

She tilted her head, looking up at him, and then she asked him honestly, "Is it, though?"

"I've always been curious about you, and so far, you've been pleasant enough."

"You were curious about me?" she asked, dubious.

"As a peccati, haven't you ever wondered about the work I do or any of the others?"

She shrugged. "I keep myself busy with my own work, and I prefer not to think of any of you at all."

"I imagine it is easier that way," Indy said. "Well, hopefully, for the wedding, we can put our differences aside and be friends."

"I can manage for a few days," she said as they arrived at the entrance of the Fabula Inn.

Indy had been carrying her luggage, but he handed it to her now. His fingertips brushed hers for only a moment, and her heart skipped a beat.

"I will see you soon, Tristitia," he said.

"Until then, take care, Industria." She turned and headed into the inn, and she could feel him watching her until she disappeared through the door.

CHAPTER NINE

AS LUX STOOD UNDER THE FLORAL ARCHWAY in the courtyard beyond the palace, he found himself feeling equal parts delight and terror.

He loved Lily completely, and he wanted to be with her forever. But he had been worried that Valefor would do something to tear them apart from the moment he met her.

The weeks since he had been living in Insontia with her had somehow been the most sublime and most stressful of his long life. Now he was mere moments from being bound with Lily forever, and his heart raced in fear that the moment would never come.

It didn't help that he couldn't see her yet. Lily was still in the palace, with Wick. A few dozen guests were seated around the archway, where Lux stood alone, waiting for his bride.

The day was warm and lovely, although dark, wispy clouds had been swirling overhead for hours, and the wind had picked up. Flower petals drifted upwards from the ground and back onto the plants and trees, and the birds above flew backwards.

The small minstrel band had begun playing softly, which meant that Lily would soon arrive. Lux smiled his most charming smile as he surveyed his guests. Many were the royal family and other nobility he'd only recently become acquainted with, like

Lily's father King Adriel and Lily's nursemaid
Nancilla – who both wept while clinging to one
another.

Aeterna the irin was there, along with Tarragon
the woodsprite, but Luminelle was unable to return to
Cormundie just yet.

The few guests there for him could hardly be
counted as family or friend, outside of Gula. He stood
at Lux's side as his best man and wore a brightly
colored floral wreath in his hair. The only other
peccati in attendance was Tris, who he barely knew.
She wore a lowcut emerald dress, and she slunk into
the back row, sitting alone.

Lux had invited everyone but Invidia and Ira, and
none of the rest had shown.

Then, finally, blessedly, he heard the unicorn, and
his Princess came from the palace. Lily rode on the
back of a black unicorn called Addonexus, both of
them adorned in flowers, and she looked ethereal and
perfect in a blue gown that flowed around her.

When her eyes met his, he felt exactly as he had
the very first time he saw her. Utterly captivated by
her beauty, and so drawn to her, he had to fight the
urge to run to her.

Astride the unicorn, she went down the aisle with
the pink blossoms from the nearby orchard raining
upwards around her.

When she reached him, Lux took her hand and
helped her down. Her skin felt soft and cool against
his, like a revitalizing rain in the desert.

Before they walked to the altar, he pulled her
close – one hand on the small of her back, the other
still holding hers. He looked into her dark eyes, so
bright and full, and he knew then, as he'd known

since the first time he'd kissed her, that he loved her more than he'd ever dreamed he could love anything. In a low voice so no one could hear but her, he said, "You are my everything. I love you today, tomorrow, and every day until the very end of time." Tears glistened in her eyes, and she tenderly touched his face. "I love you so. I cannot wait to share eternity with you."

The officiant who was presiding over the ceremony cleared his throat, since Lux and Lily were lost in each other for a moment.

"Shall we begin?" the officiant asked.

"Of course." Lux released her waist but held her hand as they walked beneath the floral archway.

The officiant read the wedding vows aloud, and then had Lux recite them back to Lily. He meant the words he was saying, but he fumbled through them because he couldn't believe it was finally happening. Lily and he would be joined together forever, and nothing could take that away from them.

Finally, the officiant asked her, "Do you Liliana Adreiella Castiline of Insontia take Maxon Eromare Regulon of Desiderium in marriage – uniting in body and soul, from now until you're dying day?"

"I do," she said in a voice loud and clear.

"With that, I pronounce you husband and wife –" the officiant was saying, but Lily didn't wait for him to finish.

She moved quickly, and her lips crashed into his. He pressed her to him and kissed her. She curled the hair at the nape of his neck around her finger.

Above them, the swirling clouds suddenly rumbled. A thunderous crack rattled through the lands. Lily and Lux parted in time to see bright blue bolts of lightning cutting jagged lines across the sky.

"Let us retire indoors before the rain comes!" the King announced.

Lux grabbed his new wife's hand, and together they ran into the palace with all their guests.

CHAPTER TEN

TRIS STOOD AT THE EDGE of the ballroom, where the post-wedding banquet was underway. She held a glass of wine in one hand, and a turkey leg in the other, which were the only two bright spots of the whole affair.

There had been so much talking and so many toasts; first the bride's father, then a handsome irin with ivory wings, and finally the Castimonia herself gave a speech, though at least hers was brief.

All of them had been so long-winded (especially the irin, it's one of the reasons she hated talking to them in general), and Tris was starving. Her stomach rumbled so loudly that other guests had looked at her.

The very moment that they were free to eat, Tris had marched straight over to the banquet table. And that's where she stayed. Eating, drinking, glaring at the jubilant guests, and once again cursing Ava.

Most everyone ignored her completely, and the other peccati were busy in their roles as groom and best man. Ava still hadn't shown his face, and Tris was beginning to fear he'd conned her into attending as some sort of prank.

She'd just taken another big bite of the turkey leg when Indy caught her eye from across the room. She felt it again – the flash of something all too recognizable – but her annoyance and frustration overwhelmed that. As he made his way over to her, she considered taking her leave because there wasn't anything for her here.

But… she didn't. She gulped down her food and took a long drink, and she waited for Indy to reach her.

"You seem to be having a good time," he said.

"The turkey legs aren't quite enough to make the long journey worthwhile, but they are delicious," she said.

He cracked a smile. "I'll be sure to try them."

"What about you?" she asked. "Was the wedding everything you hoped it would be?"

"I don't know that I really had hopes for it. It's been a nice day, and we're all safe and relatively happy, so there isn't much more I could want." He shrugged, then carefully asked, "I don't mean to sound rude, but… why did you come to the wedding?"

"Lux invited me," she said simply, avoiding the truth of Ava convincing her. "He's thrown Cormundie into such a mess, and I wanted to know what all the fuss is about."

"Now you do. What do you think?"

Tris watched the two of them – Lux and Lily – dancing together. They looked at one another with unabashed adoration, and when they kissed, she swore they both glowed.

"They love each other, that much is clear," Tris admitted. "But I do wonder if true love is worth destroying the world over."

"You think banishing Valefor is the equivalent of the destruction of the world?" Indy asked.

"The world is out of balance, and none of us know what's to come. Their star-crossed union might very well bring the end of everything we've ever known."

"Maybe," Indy agreed. "But maybe it will be the start of something better."

"It's easy for you to say when your side is winning, and your Mistress hasn't been banished." Something occurred to her, and Tris surveyed the room. "Where is Luminelle? Why isn't she here?"

He waited a beat before reluctantly answering, "It's as you said. The balance is shifting. She is not allowed onto Cormundie. Not while Valefor is gone."

"Your Mistress has been banished as well?" she asked. This was news to her, and it certainly seemed as though Luminelle's servants were trying to keep her absence a secret.

He shifted uneasily but wouldn't meet her gaze. "She hasn't referred to it that way."

"But she can't step foot on Cormundie."

"No."

"And you're not worried about what all this imbalance might mean for you?" Tris pressed.

His dark eyebrows pinched together. Although he tried to keep a passive smile on as he watched the newlyweds dance, Tris could see the corner of his mouth twitching, and his hand kept flexing-unflexing at his side.

There was a long pause as Indy searched for an answer, and when he spoke, his voice was low but strong, "I have to believe that something better is coming."

Before she could ask him anything more, Gula approached them. He was a burly man, towering over everyone else in the hall, with broad shoulders and a thick, soft belly. His dazzling green eyes paired very well with his infectious smile. Resting atop his shoulder length dark hair, he wore a crown of bright flowers. Two mugs overflowing with amber ale occupied both his hands, and he had a big goofy grin.

"By the looks of you two, I'd guess we were at a funeral," he said. "This is a *celebration*! It won't hurt you to have a little fun."

"I feel like I've been celebrating for days already," Indy said with a tired laugh.

"I hardly know a soul here," Tris said.

"Well, you only need to know one to have a partner to dance with," Gula said, motioning between the two of them with his mugs. "You know Indy, you know me." Then he gestured over to the bride and groom. "I bet Lux would even let you cut in for a dance or two."

"That seems quite rude, doesn't it?" Indy asked.

"Well, if you don't want to seem rude, you ought to ask the lady to dance," Gula suggested.

Indy opened his mouth, and Tris was certain that he would protest. Instead he looked down at her and held his hand out.

"Tristitia, may I have this dance?"

Despite herself, she smiled and took his hand. He led her out to the dancefloor, under the rusting chandeliers of the Insontian palace. When he put his hand on her waist, a delicious chill ran through her. As she put her hand on his shoulder, she noticed the subtle twitch at the corner of his mouth, like he felt it too.

They fell in step together easily, moving in the slow familiar rhythm of the ballo – a popular dance in Cormundie. It had a few simple moves, so it required very little concentration, but neither of them said anything right away.

"Have you danced much in your life?" she asked.

"Enough," he replied simply.

"*Enough?*" She smirked up at him. "Can you ever really dance enough?"

"I have danced before, and it wasn't too much, so isn't that enough?" he countered. "I hadn't realized that the Tristitia would have such a zest for life."

"I'd hardly call it a 'zest,' but long ago I came to realize that I need to enjoy life when the opportunity arises, because it doesn't arise often."

"Is that why you have such a magnificent gown?" His eyes flicked lower, and she felt the heat of his gaze as he admired her for a moment.

"I work for a King. I do have the occasion in which a gown is necessary, and I also have an eye for fine things."

His hand was cool on her lower back, his palm spread flat and wide across her as he subtly directed her movements for the ballo. They were nearer to the edge of the dancefloor, away from where the other revelers were enjoying themselves. There the music was softer, the light was dimmer.

In the crowded room, they had found a private moment. When they'd first started dancing, Indy had made sure to keep her at a respectable distance with inches between them. But as they swayed, following the slow steps of the ballo, they drew closer together.

Tris hadn't made a conscious choice to do it, but there was a *pull*, a gentle tug toward him. Their bodies pressed together ever so slightly, but she could feel his heart pounding in time with hers.

"Tris," he said, his voice low and husky. "I – "

The entrance to the ballroom suddenly opened, and hushed murmurs ran through the crowd as guests arrived late to the party. Tris pulled her gaze away from Indy's, and she looked over to see Ava and Su parting the room as they strode in.

"They're here," she said, astounded but relieved. "Avaritia and Superbia."

CHAPTER ELEVEN

WITH TRIS GONE, Sabina had been relegated to doing the consiliarius duties on top of her regular seneschal tasks. Sitting at the peccati's big desk in the chancery office felt improper, but it was as the King had commanded her to do.

She carefully opened his correspondence, making sure not to break the delicate wax seals. It was a slow, time-consuming process, but she was afraid of how His Majesty would react if she damaged anything, even the wax.

Or at least that was what Tris had taught her to say if King Dolorin commented. It gave her an excuse for taking hours to open a few letters.

One of the first concepts Tris had clarified to her when Sabina started working in the palace was something called malicious compliance.

"Desperationis is not always a kind kingdom, and the King is often reluctant to think of others," Tris had explained. "Sometimes, the King will give orders that we find cruel or unfair. We cannot and would not ever disobey him, so we comply. But we move slowly. We are perfectionists, so every task takes a very long time, and so fewer tasks can be done. Fewer injustices can be inflicted."

So that is how Sabina did her job. Slow perfectionism had worked for Tris, and it seemed to be working for the seneschal, too.

"Sabina?" Ira poked his head into the room, and it startled her so badly, she nearly jumped to her feet.

"The King told me to sit here," Sabina replied immediately, as if he'd accused her of anything.

He frowned in confusion. "Okay. Um, he just sent me to fetch you. He wants us to meet with him and Mephis in the throne room. The cauldron was bubbling."

"His cauldron bubbled?" Sabina echoed, and now her heart was racing like a terrified jackrabbit. "Is that normal?"

Still bemused, Ira laughed and shook his head. "Wouldn't you know that better than me? You've been here longer than I have."

That was true, but Sabina hadn't actually worked for King Dolorin that long. The position of seneschal had always been held by sonneillons, until Tris noticed how organized the fauns were in their community. Tris had finally convinced the King that a faun could do better than the forever-scheming sonneillons, and after an arduous audition process, Sabina had landed the job only a year ago.

Things had been smooth so far, but she kept waiting for His Royal Highness to grow tired of her or angry or disappointed. Most of the people in the capital city seemed happy or indifferent to living with the fauns, but the ones that were the most unhappy tended to be the most vocal.

In her heart, Sabina feared it would only be a matter of time until the King turned against her. But she had to stay, she had to try, because it was the only way her fellow fauns could earn any respect and any sense of comradery. She worked tirelessly to show the royalty her value, the worth of her people, and to protect the townsfolk whenever she could.

Admittedly, she didn't have much influence on the King, but as the seneschal, she had opportunities no one else from Little Faunton had. She couldn't waste it.

Like many of the nobility and practitioners of sorcery, the King had a cauldron, and she'd known about it. It was her understanding that it was used to communicate with those far away and get glimpses of the future, but her mother had always warned her that cauldrons could be dark and dangerous things.

"I haven't been around him when he's used the cauldron before," Sabina said finally. "But if he wants us there, we should hurry and not keep him waiting."

She rose quickly and smoothed out the front of her dress. An audience before the King meant she needed to look her best, and she ran her fingers through her long wavy tresses.

She and Ira walked together out of the chancery and through the dark halls of the palace. The ceilings were high, but the walls were close, and everywhere had an echo.

"You work very hard for the King," Ira said.

"Yes, of course I do." She glanced over at him. "Don't you?"

"No, I do," he agreed emphatically.

He looked about her age of twenty, maybe even a little younger. His face and his body were hard, all stocky and angular. The rest of him could've belonged to any ageless thug, but his eyes showed an earnest humanity.

Sabina hadn't expected him to be so polite. It had been impossible to not overhear him complain and argue with Tris. But with Sabina, Ira had never been anything but respectful.

"Nobody around here seems to want to work hard," Ira lamented and ran his hand through his shaggy red hair. "I became the Ira because I wanted to change the world, but Tris seems so set on just keeping Cormundie the way it always was."

"There is danger in change," she replied. "It frightens many, especially those who are prudent."

"And you? What do you think of change?" Ira was watching her, his sincere eyes studying her.

"Change is often necessary. It is okay to be frightened but fighting against it is a game in futility. I find it best to embrace change with wide eyes and clenched fists," she said.

He smiled, approving and lopsided, and he suddenly looked even younger, like a boy of sixteen. "That's my view, too."

They had reached the throne room, and their conversation – and Ira's smile – stopped at the entrance. As soon as they stepped inside, she curtseyed, even though the King had his back to them.

The throne room was much the same as the rest of the palace. So much dark stone with high ceilings. Sabina had always thought it such a strange thing that outside, the palace was lush and green, and inside, it was dark and barren. Like life encasing death.

A large chair made of carved leviathan bones sat on the dais, and the view of the capital city was blocked out with heavy velvet curtains. Sun crept in just below the hems, and the room was dimly lit by candles and the glow of the cauldron.

In the far corner of the room was a large cauldron, made from black obsidian. The liquid bubbling inside emitted a faint green glow. Both King Dolorin and Mephis were standing beside it, peering down into the cauldron. The sonneillon had returned to advise the King as soon as Tris had left to obtain the ambrosian honey.

"You summoned us, Sire?" Sabina said, and when he turned to look at her, she curtseyed again.

"I have just spoken with Valefor," the King said, and he smiled in such a prideful way, as if he thought that she would be jealous. Sabina hoped to never, ever have reason to speak with the banished daemon.

"How is our Master?" Ira asked sunnily.

"He is making the most of his time in the other realm," King Dolorin explained. "Plans are being made as he regains his strength. There are rituals that must be done, and he commanded us to prepare for them."

"What preparations?" Ira asked.

"We need to grow our stockpiles of certain foods as well as gold and iron," the King said matter-of-factly. "Desperationis must cut off all trade with any other kingdoms, and we will need to stop donating any food to our citizens."

Sabina's stomach dropped. Since Tris had been gone on His Royal Highness's command to get costly honey, Sabina alone had been left with trying to convince the King to increase his contributions. The Altering had caused disturbances in food supply, and more townsfolk than ever were struggling to get enough to eat.

Yesterday, she had managed to get the King to agree not to trade all their fruit for gold from Auctoritis. Now, just a day later, he was reversing his position completely, so there would be no food and no gold.

"But Sire, yesterday..." Sabina weakly began to argue, but the King held up his hand, silencing her.

"That doesn't matter," he said dismissively. "I hadn't talked to Valefor then. He told me to hoard all that we can. Troubled times are ahead, and we have the ritual to do. The kingdom has nothing to spare."

"Won't people starve if we do that?" Ira asked, lending his voice since Sabina couldn't find hers. He'd been there yesterday, when she had been making her impassioned arguments to the King, and he'd even joined in helping her plead her case.

"What does that matter in the face of Valefor returning?" the King asked, like he thought both Ira and the question were the most ridiculous things he'd ever heard. "People will die in order for our Master to return. We've always known that. But when he returns, he will take his rightful place and share with us all his glory. We'll want for nothing. If the price is the kingdom suffering now, so be it."

Sabina lowered her eyes, staring down at her hooves poking out underneath her dress. The King had made his decision, on the whims of an absent daemon, and nothing could make him care about how that would hurt his own people.

"What do you need me to do?" she asked softly, because there was no argument that he would hear.

The King rattled a list of tasks involving redirecting their food supplies and increasing their storage.

As he spoke, the wind outside gathered speed, and the curtains billowed. Through the gaps in the fabric, Sabina could see the clouds darkening the sky, and the air had an icy chill to it.

"I've given you enough to do already," the King said as he finished. "Now, go on and hurry. We need to begin as soon as possible."

Sabina curtseyed, and Ira bowed more slowly. They both exited the throne room to fulfill his callous orders.

"How bad do you think it will be?" Ira asked her, once they were out in the hall, away from the King and Mephis's ears. "For the kingdom, if the King reserves all the food."

She shook her head, because she didn't know and she didn't want to think about it. "I'll do all that I can."

"What does that mean?" He lowered his voice, just above a whisper. "Will you disobey the King?"

"Wouldn't you run and tell him if I did?" she countered.

"The King isn't my Master. Valefor is."

"But he is following Valefor's wishes."

"I'll help the King gather what he needs for the ritual, but he doesn't need to hoard everything," Ira said. "If you and I work together, I think we can find a way to serve Valefor without everyone starving to death."

"You really think it will be that easy?" she asked him dubiously.

"Probably not, but we can still try."

"How did you come to work for your Master?" Sabina asked.

It wasn't the first time that she had wondered that, but it was the first time she had the courage to actually ask. Ira was going to defy the King to help others, and that made it difficult for her to reconcile him being the very embodiment of wrath.

"I grew up in an orphanage over in the kingdom of Furorem," he explained. "They kicked me out onto the streets, and I was never much good at anything but brawling with the other boys. I ended up bare-knuckle fighting as a pugilist, and I was doing all right for myself."

A strange smile quirked on his mouth, somehow vacillating between pride and shame. "I was really good at it, honestly, and I started making serious coin.

"But others took notice," he said with a sigh. "An ogre pulverized me after a fight. He stole all my money and left me bleeding in an alley."

Sabina gasped. "That's horrible!"

He nodded once, solemn. "It was. But Mephis found me, and he asked me if I wanted to be powerful enough that no one could ever do that to me again. I said yes, and he brought me to meet with Valefor… and you know the rest."

He'd barely finished his sentence when thunder clapped so loudly it rattled everything around them. Outside, the wind roared.

They were still on the highest floor of the palace, and Sabina ran to the balcony that wrapped around the south side. The hall floor leading to it was slick with rain cascading in. It was as if the sky had opened up and dumped the sea upon them.

Through the open archway, she could see the devastation. The clouds swirled with debris – green leaves, broken boards, even the odd harpy goblin – and torrential rain poured down.

Sabina was frozen, watching in horror until Ira grabbed her hand.

"It's not safe here!" He was shouting to be heard over the roar of the wind. "We have to go inside!" He pulled her away just as a palm tree flipped over the balcony and flew past her. It crashed into the wall, the wood shattering like glass.

That was all the convincing she needed. She squeezed his hand, and the two of them raced deeper into the palace to survive the storm.

CHAPTER TWELVE

INDY HAD NEVER MET THESE PARTICULAR Avaritia and Superbia, but he recognized them before Tris told him.

They were crashing a Princess's wedding, and yet they strode in like they were the most important ones. In a room that held a King, many nobles, a witch, and an irin.

Ava was tall and lean, wearing an exquisite suit the color of a ripened plum. He had the calculating eyes of a feral cat, and even his lazy smirk had a feline quality to it. But it was his jewelry that truly caught the eye – glittering gemstones on every finger and on chains around his neck. His long hair was pulled back, off his face.

Beside him, Superbia was not to be outshone. Her gown was made of lavish lace and velvet in the colors of the sunset – shimmering copper to blazing orange. Her skin was pale, contrasting with her long black hair.

When her eyes scanned the room, she was annoyed, but her heart-shaped lips turned into a full-on scowl when they landed on Wick standing next to the King.

Wick had mentioned that years ago she'd worked for Superbia, and it hadn't been a happy experience. By the look on Superbia's face, Indy gathered it had been mutually unpleasant.

"*Finally*," Tris said with a sigh of relief.

She was still in Indy's arms, even though they had stopped dancing, and when he looked down at her, she was smiling at Ava.

He felt a pang of something – not jealousy, he doesn't feel that way, and certainly not about someone he'd only met the day before. But it was a pain, a small twist inside his heart when Tris happily hurried off to greet Ava and Su.

Of course she'd rather be with her fellow peccati than him, and the reverse should be true for him, as well, so it was nothing to worry on. But still he did.

He followed after Tris to intercept Ava and Su before they could reach Lily. Indy had known that Lux invited them, but he had not truly expected them to show up. Now that they had, Indy didn't trust their motives, and he wanted to keep them away from Lily as much as he could.

"Why are you so late?" Tris was demanding of Ava as Indy joined them. "You *promised* you'd meet me here."

"And I am here now." Ava put his hand on her shoulder, comforting her, and Indy felt that twist in his chest again.

Tris frowned, and Ava dropped his hand to his side and offered her an apologetic smile.

"Su took some convincing," he said, passing the blame onto his compatriot.

"I prefer to be fashionably late anyway," Su said, and she looked over at Indy. "Who is this serious man shadowing you, Tris?"

"He's Indy, the Industria."

Su recoiled slightly, then she smirked. "Of course he is."

"You made it!" Lux shouted exuberantly as he rushed over to greet them. "I can't believe you actually made it!"

When he reached them, Ava held out his hand for a handshake, but Lux pulled him in for a hug.

"*Oh!*" Ava exclaimed in surprise. "I didn't realize we were hugging now."

"It's my wedding day, and I'm happy," Lux said as he released them. "Why shouldn't we hug?"

Su held up her hand when Lux faced her. "I am going to pass on any of the embracing."

"Thank you for coming, Su," Lux said. "It's good to see you again."

"Is that her over there?" Su asked, looking past him to where Lily and Wick were talking. "The virtu who stole your heart?"

Lux beamed. "Yes. That's *my wife*. I can introduce you, if you'd like."

"Why rush it?" Indy blurted out, because he couldn't think of a reason to keep Ava and Su away from Lily.

At that moment he was acutely aware that he was surrounded by peccati, and Lily was a novice virtu in a precarious situation.

"You've only just arrived," Indy went on, forcing a smile at them. "Why don't you eat and drink first?"

"We actually ate and drank plenty in our carriage ride down," Ava said and patted his belly.

"Is that Wick she's talking to?" Su asked, with her narrowed eyes locked on Lily and Wick.

"Yes, it is," Lux said.

"I used to know her, some years ago," Su said. "But she's so *old* now."

"Humans age, Su," Ava reminded her dryly. "You've always known that."

"What about you?" Su asked Lux. "Will you age now? Are you just a mortal man again?"

"Not exactly," Lux said, and he cast a glance at all the guests looking on. "It is quite loud in here with the minstrel band. Why don't we go somewhere else, where it's quieter so we can all catch up?"

"Sounds perfect," Ava said, and Lux darted away to get Gula before they all went off together.

Tris looked to Indy. "What about you? Are you joining us?"

He nodded. "Yes." He didn't want to leave Lily alone, but he could not ignore a meeting of the peccati.

Lux led the way through the palace, winding down a few corridors until they reached the covered courtyard. Outside, it had begun to rain, and through the skylight, the same blue lightning from earlier in the day continued zagging across the night sky. Out here, it was far from the wedding festivities, and other than the sound of the rain and distant thunder, it was quiet.

Indy, Tris, Ava, Su, Lux, and Gula stood in a loose circle, and the earlier pretense of cheer had evaporated into the ether.

"You haven't answered my question yet, *Luxuria*," Su said pointedly.

"You asked if I'm just a mortal man," Lux said as he rolled up his sleeves. He held up his hands and flames licked out from his fingertips.

"So you can make fire, but can you die?" Su asked, sounding bored and annoyed.

"All I know for certain is that I haven't died yet," Lux replied.

"You're awfully curious about Lux for someone who didn't even want to come here," Ava said.

"I never said I wasn't curious about anything," Su snapped at him. *"Obviously* I have questions. None of us have any idea what the hell is happening, or what it means for our future. What I said is that this is a waste of time because we won't find any of the answers that we want."

"There's only one question that we need to answer tonight," Tris said. "What is to be done about Valefor?"

None of them said anything. Ava looked to Lux, who stared grimly at the ground, and Su clicked her tongue in irritation.

"If Valefor returns, he is going to kill me and my wife," Lux said. "I plan to do everything in my power to stop him."

"But what exactly is in your power?" Su asked skeptically. "You and the fledgling Castimonia? What can you do to stop Valefor?"

"We banished him in the first place," Lux countered defensively.

Su rolled her eyes. "Don't pretend like that was some careful plot that you two schemed up."

"Maybe not," Lux allowed. "But we still banished him, for the first time in eons. Plenty of others plotted and planned to rid Cormundie of him, and they all failed."

"This was the first time his peccati went against him," Tris said. "All the other attempts at overthrowing Valefor were by his enemies on the outside. Kings, sorcerers, ogres, dragons, and the like."

"So…" Indy spoke carefully and eyed up the daemon's minions that surrounded him. "Do any of you hope for Valefor's return?"

Ava laughed, and Su's face contorted up in disgust. Tris just shook her head, as did Gula and Lux, but Indy already knew how they felt. Still, he was surprised that so many of Valefor's closest minions were so ready to turn on their Master.

He had never imagined being able to forsake his own Mistress. Although, he supposed, that so many of the things happening lately had been far beyond his imagination.

"We all have things we'd rather be doing than running ridiculous and dangerous errands for a mercurial immortal," Su elaborated, so Indy's shock must've been evident on his face. "I prefer how I spend my time to be decided by me and me *alone*."

"What about the other two peccati?" Indy asked.

"Invidia thinks he'll have more power if Valefor returns, so he's working toward that," Ava said.

"And Ira's dead," Lux added, glancing over at Ava as he did.

"No, there's a *new* Ira," Tris corrected him, and Lux's eyes widened. "Valefor already replaced him and sent the new Ira to me to mentor him."

"Why did he choose you?" Su asked.

"Are you jealous? Do you want to take Ira under your wing?" Tris asked. "He's an angry nightmare, and he's all yours."

"No, I just don't know why Valefor would pick you—"

"It doesn't matter," Ava said, cutting through the bickering. "Ira's here now, and he's working to bring Valefor back. As is Invidia. What are we going to do to stop them?"

"I might not want Valefor to return," Su said. "But I am not willing to give up *any* of my powers. I have earned what I have, and I will not relinquish it."

A squawking noise chirped from the ceiling, and they all looked up. At first, Indy didn't see anything, but when the lightning flashed again, he spotted it – an oculatu. It was one of the winged-eyeball goblins that spied for the sonneillons.

Su shrieked when she saw it. "I knew this was a terrible idea!"

"I can get it!" Gula shouted, and he lunged at the goblin, jumping high in the air. The little monster was faster, and it flew out into the rain, beyond his long grasp.

Gula ran after it, assuring the others he could catch any goblin, but Su was not about to wait around to see if he could. She shook her head and stormed back into the palace, with Ava rushing right behind her.

But Tris just stared up in the darkness, at the shadows where the oculatu had been hiding

CHAPTER THIRTEEN

IT WAS LATE IN THE NIGHT when Tris gathered her cloak and headed toward the palace door. She'd stayed at the reception much later than she meant to, later than she even wanted.

After the oculatu interrupted the meeting of the peccati, everyone had been spooked. Even Lux, who hadn't seemed like anything could dampen his joy, had been more subdued when they returned to the ballroom. Both he and Indy hovered close to Lily, as if Valefor would appear any moment and snatch her away.

Tris stayed at the edge of the festivities, sipping her amber ale and hoping that Ava and Su would return. But they never did.

Ordinarily, Tris disliked spending any time with her brethren. They were often selfish, arrogant, and cruel, and it was best if they avoided one another.

But now they were the only ones she had to stand beside her against their Master. She couldn't decide what was worse – that she had to rely on Ava and Su, or that they had fled at the first sign of danger.

At any rate, the wedding celebration was drawing to a close, and Tris had no reason to be there. There would be no more plotting against Valefor tonight.

She wrapped her cloak around her shoulders, and she slipped out of the ballroom. But before she made it to the exit, Indy called after her.

"You're sneaking off without a goodbye?"

When she turned back, a soft smile played on his lips, and he approached her. The subtle hint of happiness contrasted with his ever-serious eyes, but she found that she quite liked the combination.

"I didn't think anyone would notice," she said honestly.

"Are you going back to the inn?"

She nodded. "It's been a very long day, and I'm looking forward to a night's rest."

"Are you walking alone?"

"Since I am alone, I had thought I would."

"Let me walk with you," he said. His solemn gray eyes held hers for a moment, then they flicked down to the plunge of her neckline for a split second. "It's late, you're in an unfamiliar kingdom, and the oculatu have been about. It wouldn't be safe for you to go alone."

"I suppose I would fare better with a guide, in case I lose my way again," she said, and he smiled.

He grabbed his overcoat, and he held the palace door open for her. It was cooler in Insontia than it was back home in Desperationis, and the air felt heavy with a cold mist. Tris pulled her cloak more tightly around her, and they walked across the palace grounds toward the surrounding city.

"Did you have a nice time tonight?" he asked after a while.

"Nice enough," she said absently, because as they'd been walking, she'd been replaying the night's events, and something occurred to her.

"I've attended a few weddings and –" Indy was saying when she interrupted.

"Do you still have your powers?" she asked suddenly because she couldn't focus on small talk when there were greater concerns.

Indy was taken aback. "*What*?"

"What abilities do virtus have anyway?" she pressed on. "The peccati, we can all conjure fire –" she flicked a flame out from her fingertips to prove it "– and then we have other ones tuned with our natures. But I never understood what the virtus could do."

"It's about the same for us." Indy held up his hand, palm out, and as he slowly moved his hand forward, a wind grew up behind them. "We conjure air and wind." He dropped his hand and shrugged as the wind subsided.

"What else can you do?" Tris asked, looking up at him curiously.

He let out a heavy sigh. "I've inherited a handful of traits that make me stronger and more effective than the average human, but nothing so great as to call a 'power.'"

"What do you mean?" she asked.

"Other than the wind and immortality, it's nothing glamorous," he explained. "Superior strength, energy, and stamina, and a work ethic that borders on obsessive. Oh, and unicorns usually like me."

"You make yourself sound like a racehorse," she said. He actually laughed at that, a quiet rumbling deep in his chest, and the sound made her heart flutter.

"I feel like one sometimes," he admitted. "Do racehorses have frequent bouts of insomnia?"

"I don't know, but I doubt it," she said.

"So do I," he concurred, but there was a sadness in his words that she didn't understand.

"You wouldn't mind, would you?" she asked. "If we have to lose our respective powers, as they were, to stop Valefor. You'd gladly give it all up."

"I don't know that anybody 'gladly' gives up immortality," he disagreed, catching her off guard. "But I've always done what needs to be done. Rescinding my identity as a virtu would be no different."

"That's very noble," she said.

He smiled at her, but it was strained and melancholy, and she wished she could make him laugh again. "Virtus are *always* noble." Then he looked away. "What about you and the others? Will you give it up so easily?"

"I shouldn't speak for the others," she said. "But no. It won't be easy to convince all seven of us to give up anything."

"So you're not optimistic about thwarting Valefor's return?"

"I'm never optimistic," she said. "But sometimes sacrifices need to be made, and I've always been willing to make them."

"Lux has been telling me that he wanted to enlist his brethren to help us. I didn't think that would be a real option." He slowed to a stop as they reached the inn. "But you have been a very pleasant surprise, Tristitia."

She smiled at him. "You haven't been entirely unpleasant either, Industria."

"They're having a breakfast tomorrow at the palace," Indy said. "All the guests are invited. You should come. We can discuss more what we need to do."

Tris suddenly had the strongest urge to kiss him goodnight, like they were old lovers. But they were strangers at best, and enemies at worst.

But that didn't feel true to her either. When she looked into his eyes, it was not an enemy or even a

friend that she saw. It was something else,
something... *visceral*.

It was without hesitation that she answered, "Yes.
I will see you at breakfast tomorrow."

"Tomorrow then."

"Goodnight," she said, and he waited outside,
watching to make sure she made it inside safely.

CHAPTER FOURTEEN

LILY LET HIM CARRY HER over the threshold, and she couldn't help but giggle. The entire day had been like some enchanting dream, and the only proper response to this much love and happiness was to laugh.

Her husband, Maxon Eromare Regulon the new Prince of Insontia, set her down gently on the floor of their new bedroom.

With her marriage, Lily had given up her childhood bedroom in exchange for the second master. It was much larger than her previous room, and more exquisitely decorated. Wick and Nancilla had transformed it as a wedding present, but this was her first time taking it in, since they'd wanted it as a surprise.

The walls were covered in a shimmery wallpaper of ivory with silvery blue designs swirling on it. It was a subtle pattern, with butterflies mixed in with the filigree. The four-post bed was silhouetted in sheer curtains with satin bedspreads, and flower petals were sprinkled across the lush carpets.

"This is so very perfect." She beamed up at her husband. "*You* have been so very perfect."

This was no exaggeration. Throughout the entire day, she found herself looking over at him and all she could think about was how much she loved him, and how much she couldn't wait to get him alone in their marital bed.

Since their vows, she had taken to calling him Maxon. That was the name of the man she'd married, and he was so much more than his position as Luxuria. Especially since he wasn't even Lux, not anymore.

Neither of them were their title or their role, not when they were together. He was Maxon, she was Lily, and they were in love, and that's all that mattered.

When Maxon looked at her, his blue eyes twinkling, his mouth upturned in the widest of smiles, she could see how much he loved her. It was like when the day had been cold, and the sun came out. The feeling of the beams of light slowly warming her skin... that was how she felt whenever he looked at her.

On top of all that, he was the most handsome man she had ever met. His hair was light blond, cascading over his forehead when he kissed her. His shoulders were broad, his arms strong, his skin like fire.

Between them was a tether, something just beyond her touch, but Lily knew it was there as much as she knew the stars and the air were there. It was a palpable thing, a primeval *pull*. His body tilted toward her whenever they were near, and she found it hard to resist doing the same.

But now they were in their room, alone, and Maxon had locked the door behind him. There was no need to resist any longer.

He had taken off his jacket while she admired the room. She ran to him and leapt into his arms, and he caught her easily, the way she knew he always would.

Their lips crashed together in an excited kiss. His arms held her firm, but she felt his hands already working at the corset on the back of her dress.

"There's no need for that," she said.

"You are planning to keep your dress on tonight?" he asked, sounding puzzled.

She laughed. "No, but I wanted it off quickly." He set her down then, and she stepped back from him because she needed a bit of room.

"I didn't want us spending the entire wedding night with you helping me out of all my garments," Lily explained as she unfastened the few hooks hidden along the seam down her side. "I had a very awkward conversation with Nancilla, but she understood and sewed me in a quick escape."

Maxon stared at her with wide eyes, his mouth slightly agape as he watched her hurriedly undress. "I am so happy that I married such a clever woman."

With her dress loosened, she slid it off her arms and past her hips, then she let it fall to the floor where it pooled at her feet. That left her in a sheer white shift and the flowers in her long hair.

She stepped out of the dress, moving slow and deliberate, and Maxon immediately closed the distance between them. He dropped to his knees before her, and he put one hand on her waist.

The other hand went underneath her shift, on her bare skin, sliding up her thigh. His head was at her naval, and he kissed her stomach, his lips hot through the sheer cotton. His mouth slowly traveled south.

"I love you so much, Lily," he said in a husky voice between kisses. "I am so happy to be your servant for the rest of our days." Another kiss, and he was using his hands to push up her shift over her hips, leaving her skin exposed. "I want to worship at your feet every night until the very end of time."

He kissed her once more, his head bowed low to reach her intimate spots, and the tender movements of his mouth made her moan.

Then he looked up at her, a hungry smile on his lips. "Today, when I vowed to be yours, I meant it. I am yours completely, in all of my being, for all of time, my life belongs to you."

She reached down, running her fingers through his thick hair. "Then Maxon, my darling, please take me to bed."

Afterwards, their hands entwined as they lay on their backs and caught their breath, Lily noticed the mural painted on the ceiling. It was a gorgeous blue sky with fluffy clouds in pastel shades of pink and purple, like during a beautiful sunset.

"We really are so fortunate, aren't we?" Lily asked. "We found each other, we're living in this beautiful palace, we're not beholden to any master."

"Well, you have a Mistress with Luminelle," Maxon reminded her gently.

"Yes, that's true, but she's given me a great deal of freedom." Lily rolled over onto her side, so she could look him in the face. "We have more happiness than any two people could possibly deserve."

He arched an eyebrow. "Is that a complaint?"

"No, no, of course not," she said with a laugh. "But since we have so much, we really ought to share. We need to help others."

"That sounds wonderful," he agreed. "But what does that mean? Who do you want to help? How can we help them?"

"I don't know. I don't know how, I suppose," she realized. "We can talk to my father and Nancilla and

Wick. They would have good ideas about what to do. Or maybe we could talk to the townspeople."

"You want to go around the kingdom and ask people if they need help?" Maxon asked.

"I hadn't meant it quite that literally, but now that you say it, why can't we?" she countered. "We could go to neighborhoods bringing gifts of cheeses and fruits, and then we can talk to them. We can find out what they need."

"I don't know if it could be that simple," he said.

"Why couldn't it?" she asked, and she was growing more excited as she thought about it. "We'll bring gifts, and we'll talk. We are the Prince and Princess of Insontia, and someday, we'll rule this kingdom. We ought to get to know the people we're about to lord over, don't you think?"

He thought for a minute, then nodded. "You spent so much of your youth locked up in the palace, it is time you get to know Insontia and Cormundie."

"Exactly!" She kissed him again in her excitement, and he put an arm around her, hugging her close to him.

"But can we enjoy our honeymoon before we go on this charitable journey?" Maxon asked.

Instead of answering him, Lily kissed him more deeply and climbed on top of him.

CHAPTER FIFTEEN

INDY SAT AT THE LONG TABLE in the palace dining hall, surrounded by other friends and guests of the wedding. He had been among the first to arrive, and he had taken the seat closest to the door. Every time it opened, he'd look up expectantly, but so far, it had only been other guests or servants bringing in covered platters of fruit and pastries.

His stomach rumbled, but he hardly noticed. He should be worrying about the meeting of the peccati last night and what it meant for the future of Cormundie. He certainly was, but now his thoughts kept venturing back to Tris.

Before Luminelle tasked him with mentoring Lily, she had warned him of what may come. He had been at her palace in the clouds, and they were alone, walking through her tranquil conservatory.

Even in the bright room, her tawny skin seemed to radiate with light and love. Her long black hair shimmered like satin, hanging down her back between her ivory wings.

"Valefor has been banished, but the war is not over yet," Luminelle had explained. "He's lost Luxuria, but he still has time to bring others into his fold. It will be harder for him since he's trapped in his realm away from the world.

"But those who serve him still can visit, the same way you visit me," she went on. "He is removed, but not powerless, and he will be doing all he can to return to Cormundie and continue the fight."

"How can he return?" Indy asked.

"There are few ways," she replied carefully, as she paused to inspect a wilting green orchid. "The simplest one is to kill Lux and replace him with a new Luxuria who is bound to Valefor. But that would only reset the balance.

"To create an advantage, he will go after a virtu, with the goal of bringing them to his side. Lily is the most vulnerable because she's so young and so new to her role," Luminelle said as she moved on from the plant, now fully rejuvenated by her touch.

"But Lily has already defied Valefor, and that was before she fully understood what she was," Indy reasoned, strolling behind his Mistress. "With my guidance, she should be even more resistant to him."

"Valefor only had her in his grasp for a short period of time," she countered. "That was before he knew the effect she had on Lux. Now that he is aware of their connection, their strength can become their weakness, if he uses them against one another."

"Do you really think he'll be able to turn her away?" Indy asked.

"To save Lux… Perhaps, perhaps not." She stopped, her lips pressing into a thin line. "Or Valefor may just kill them both and be rid of them."

Luminelle turned to face him and put her hand tenderly on his cheek. "You have been the strongest of my children, Industria. I need you to keep the world safe until I can return to it."

"I will do all that I can," he had promised her then.

Since arriving in Insontia, he had tried to live up to his promise. Nearly every waking moment was spent preparing Lily and ensuring that she and Lux were safe.

And then he had met Tris, lost on the busy street. Her chestnut hair had been pulled up, but it was coming free, with a lock falling across her face. He'd wanted to brush it back so he could see her eyes better – green eyes bright and brilliant, like a gemstone glittering in the sunlight. Even dusty and exhausted, as she had clearly been, her face had held such beauty. A sincerity to her wide mouth, and the subtlest hint of freckles on the rose of her cheeks.

When he had managed to pull her eyes from her face, he'd noticed the rest of her. Her blouse was cut low enough to show cleavage, her small bosom accentuated by the corset snug around her waist.

She had captivated him the moment he saw her. The more time he spent with her, the more she burrowed her way into his thoughts. Last night, when he should've been sleeping, he'd been lying awake, worrying that she wasn't safe in the inn. He wished he'd invited her to the palace, with its many guest rooms and guards.

When he heard slow footfalls on the floor outside the dining hall breakfast, somehow, he knew it was her. He lifted his head in time to see Tris walking into the room.

Unlike the other women in attendance, she wore pants with an evergreen jacket. Her chestnut hair was pulled back, and she chewed her lip as she warily surveyed the room. She paused, hesitating, but then her eyes landed on him, and she broke out in a relieved smile.

He rose to greet her, like she was a princess instead of a peccati, but none of the other guests

95

seemed to notice the impropriety of it. Insontia was a more relaxed kingdom than most.

"I hope I'm not too late," she said as he motioned to the chair across from him.

"Everyone is still eating, so you're fine," he said. That was true, although he hadn't really been so much eating as picking at his fruit.

"Good," she said and began filling up her plate. "I invited Ava to the breakfast, but he said he'd rather shove hot pokers in his eyes than get out of bed."

Indy took a drink of his pomegranate juice and tried to ignore the twist in his chest again. "When… did you see Ava?"

"Last night," she said. "He was in his room at the inn, drinking and lamenting how things went. Su was frightened and ran back home."

"She's not on our side, then?" he asked, focusing on what mattered and not wondering what Tris was doing in Ava's room last night.

"*Our* side?" Tris asked with a quirked eyebrow, but her smile was playful.

"Are we not on the same side?" he asked.

"We are," she agreed. "But it will take some time for me to get used to. After so long as enemies, it's an adjustment."

"It's strange that we've been enemies for ages, and yet we'd never met before the other day."

She ate breads slathered with jams and honey, and she waited until she chewed it to speak. "I was busy with my work, and you were busy with yours. They kept us on opposite sides of Cormundie."

At the other end of the table, the King was chatting loudly with Lily, Lux, and other nearby guests. Indy had been hearing bits of their conversation throughout breakfast, but now the King was speaking louder, and he was looking down the table, toward Indy and Tris.

"Are any of you from Desperationis?" King Adriel asked, nearly shouting by then.

Tris glanced uncertainly around, then slowly lifted her hand. "I am, Sir."

"Ah, yes, *Trista*," the King said, mispronouncing her name. "How do you think your kingdom will make do?"

"Beg pardon?" she asked, confused.

"With the terrible procello that hit Desperationis," King Adriel explained.

She went pale and set down her fork. "What?"

Living on the edge of the sea, dangerous weather was never uncommon, but extremely destructive types were fortunately very rare. A procello was an incredibly vicious kind of storm, with high winds building up over the sea until they crashed into the land. Whole cities had been wiped out during a single procello.

"Yes, the storm hit yesterday afternoon, and I've gotten word from other kingdoms that the Desperationis capital city got the brunt of it," he said.

"Oh," Tris said, and then she abruptly stood up. "Thank you for all your hospitality, but I must return home." She looked over at Lux. "I need your horse."

CHAPTER SIXTEEN

VELOX WAS A BLACK STEED purported to be the fastest in the land, and Tris had once witnessed Lux racing him, so she had seen firsthand how fast the horse could run.

With the procello hitting her home, she had to get back. She'd left King Dolorin with only a new Ira and that scheming sonneillon Mephis in a disaster.

Back when she had been serving under the late King Dolian, she had once tried to take a more passive role in a time of crisis. Tris had already grown weary of advocating for suffering, so she thought if she backed off, perhaps Dolian could find a gentler way of ruling.

But she had been horribly wrong, and the massacre that followed was now a brutal reminder of what could happen if the Kings were left to their own machinations.

Not to mention her home and roommate Reni were on the Vespertine Sea. Tris had no idea how they were faring, and she needed to get back to them.

Lux offered aide without question, without asking for a favor back, so maybe the Castimonia had changed him. He led her out to the stables with his new bride and Indy in tow.

Tris had rented a carriage here, but that took her on the Great South Road that spanned the southern end of Cormundie. It went below the treacherous Austeriuga Mountains and the desolate Morsenea

Desert, which made it much less dangerous but also much, much slower.

To return quickly, she'd need a fast horse to make it through the mountain pass and across the desert.

"What is your next fastest horse?" Indy asked while Tris, Lux, and a stable hand hurried to saddle Velox and ready him for a long ride.

Lux gave Indy a quizzical look, then motioned behind him to Lily. She was in her lovely dress, unmindful of the train dragging through manure and mud.

"Lily, which of your father's horses is the fastest?" Lux asked.

She paused, glancing about. "None of them are as quick as yours. But I know of one that is." With that, she turned and dashed out of the stable.

"Why are you asking?" Tris eyed Indy over the back of the horse. "Are you running back to your kingdom to make sure it's still standing?"

"I'm going with you," Indy said. "King Adriel claimed that storm decimated your home. I presume you'll need all the help you can get."

She was surprised – when has a virtu ever helped a peccati? But Indy was right, and strange times often lead to strange bedfellows.

"Thank you," Tris said simply.

A minute later, Lily returned, leading in the ebony unicorn she'd ridden in the wedding yesterday. He was an immense beast with a glittering horn, and he surveyed them with intelligent eyes.

"This is Addonexus, and he may even be faster than Velox," Lily explained as she introduced the unicorn to Indy. "Addonexus, this is my friend, Indy. He needs help getting to Desperationis."

Indy let the great animal sniff him before gently
petting his snout. "Hello, Addonexus."

The unicorn chuffed and looked back at Lily, and
the Princess assured him that he was in good hands.

"We'll send aide for you as soon as we can," Lily
said once they were all saddled up and ready to go.

"Lily, should you make a promise like that?" Lux
asked. "Your father is still the King, and
Desperationis isn't exactly friendly with Insontia."

"That is a problem for us to sort out," Lily said,
and she looked up at Tris astride Lux's horse. "I will
do all I can to help you. When you arrive in
Desperationis, send me word of what your people
need."

Tris nodded. "Thank you, Lily."

Then, because she didn't want to waste any more
time, she spurred the horse on. Indy rode Addonexus
beside her, and together, they raced through the
rolling hills of Insontia.

They didn't talk while they rode, and they only
stopped when necessary. They rode through the first
night, only taking breaks for an hour here and there to
let the animals eat and rest, and they made it through
the narrow mountain pass.

The sun was starting to set on the second day
when they stopped between rivers near the borders of
Voracitis and Desperationis. Tris and Indy were close
enough to the capital city of Voracitis that they could
see the lamps glowing and smell the sweet pastries
and savory meats.

Her plan had been to stop in Voracitis on her way
back on the Great South Road, which went by the
Apisius Valley where she could procure the pricey
ambrosian honey for King Dolorin. That was the
whole reason he had allowed her to leave in the first

place, since he'd never have let her attend the Luxuria's betrayal of a wedding.

But she didn't have time for that now. Venturing to the Apisius Valley, even on a fast horse like Velox, would still add at least a day to her already lengthy journey. King Dolorin would be enraged when she returned empty-handed, but she had faced his anger before and survived. The kingdom of Desperationis was her main concern.

Tris stood at the river's edge, stretching her aching legs and staring ahead at the western horizon, towards her home. Behind her, the horse and unicorn were grazing, and Indy was tending to them.

"We should rest here tonight," Indy said.

She stiffened but didn't look at him. "I'm needed home now."

"I know, but the animals need a break." He came up beside her, but she still wouldn't look at him. "I don't think it's safe for us to be travelling the Morsenea Desert at night. Especially not when the weather and the world are so… in flux."

Most of Desperationis was covered in a vast desert wasteland, between the coast to the west and the Demius River to the east. It was not an easy journey, even in the best of circumstances, with sand leviathans and hungry vultures. The days were hot and unrelenting, the nights were cold and hostile.

"You cannot help anyone if you don't make it home alive," Indy said, more gently this time.

She sighed and surrendered. "We can make camp nearby and leave at first light."

"There's a nice spot under the willow tree just up the riverbank over there," he said, motioning behind them.

She looked back and saw he'd already started gathering sticks for a fire and cleared an area for them.

They'd both packed lightly, with thin blankets spread out on the ground. Indy had smartly grabbed some bread, cheese, and wine, and he shared with her beside the fire.

"Thank you for all of this," Tris said as she ripped off hunks of bread and tossed them in her mouth.

"No one should make the journey alone when their home is in peril."

"I suppose I should not be surprised by kindness from a virtu," she said.

"Is there not much kindness in Desperationis?" he asked.

Tris gave him a sidelong glance. "Have you never been to the kingdom before?"

"Luminelle keeps us to the east of Valefor's lair, but I've passed through the Morsenea Desert once or twice," he said. "I never stayed for long."

"I imagine that Desperationis is the same as anywhere else in Cormundie. The wicked are cruel, the innocent are kind, but most fall in between trying to survive," she said.

Indy looked at her from across the flame, the amber light dancing in his dark eyes. "I'm sorry. I never mean to speak disparagingly about anyone. I know you have friends there."

Her thoughts went to Reni, the faun seneschal Sabina, and the other commonfolk she encountered every day. She even thought of Ira, who was more trouble than he was worth, but she didn't want to see harm unnecessarily come to him.

But her mind didn't linger there too long. A fog of exhaustion was rolling over her, and she lay back on the hard ground.

"We'll sleep now and rise early," she said. Above her, the stars swirled beyond the tree branches, and her heavy lids started to close.

"I'll keep watch for danger," Indy promised as she drifted off.

CHAPTER SEVENTEEN

INDY KNEW HE SHOULD FOLLOW HER lead and take his own advice. He should sleep, he should rest, but he couldn't, so he didn't.

He watched Tris slumber, peaceful and lovely in the firelight, and that did little to ease his anxious mind.

He feared that he left Lily – and by extension, Lux – under protected, and he worried on his own willingness to leave them so easily. Was this a trick? Was it Valefor's meddling that compelled him to travel with Tris?

Or was it the stricken look in her eyes when King Adriel told her of the procello?

Indy had been warned his whole life about what selfish beings the peccati were, how they could never truly care for another. But he had seen it on her face – the terror and desperation as she looked off at her homeland far in the distance.

There was far more to Tris than he'd been told was possible, and he felt something for her he never thought he could feel: understanding, fondness, attraction.

None of this made sense. Maybe it was the madness of Cormundie. The vacuum left in the absence of Valefor and Luminelle had changed the world, and maybe it had changed Tris, too. The Altering made everything off-kilter and precarious.

His legs felt restless, despite the aches of the day, so he got up and gathered supplies. Fruit and nuts from the trees, and water from the river for their canteens.

Eventually, when he'd busied himself with all he could think to do, Indy gave into pacing. Back and forth in the shadows, under the ever-moving stars, he walked and chewed his thumbnail.

"Indy?" Tris asked groggily, interrupting his loop of thoughts. "Is everything okay?"

"Yes, I just wanted to be sure we had everything we need for tomorrow," he said.

"Do we?"

"Yes."

She propped herself up on her elbow to look at him better, studying him over the dwindling embers of the fire. "Are you going to rest now?"

He exhaled roughly. "I have insomnia."

"I can help with that," she offered.

He shook his head. "I am accustomed to it. I'll be all right."

"Now is no time to be stubborn. It's as you told me. Tomorrow will be arduous, and you need to be rested. The sand leviathans should be sleeping this time of year, but everything is different now, so we must be on guard." She patted the blanket beside her, and her emerald eyes were beseeching as she gazed up at him. "Let me help you."

He nodded, not because she was right – although, she was – but simply because it was what he wanted. He *wanted* to sit beside her, to let her comfort him.

"Lie down," she commanded when he sat on the blanket next to her.

So he did. He gritted his teeth and blinked up at the sky, trying to still himself.

Tris moved, so she was kneeling beside him, and then her head came into view, blocking out the stars.

For a moment, he thought she might kiss him, and his breath caught in his throat. But she only smiled sadly at him.

"Have you ever let go for a moment in your whole life?" she asked.

"Let go of what?" he asked.

"*Anything.*"

She ran her hand through his hair, and it sent a shiver through him.

"When I was a young child, my mother used to tell me bedtime stories about the lands we lived on," she said, her voice soft and gentle. "Would you like me to tell you one now? They always helped me sleep."

"Yes," he replied, because he wanted to hear her voice as she stroked his hair.

"I will tell you a story, and when I'm done, you'll have the best sleep of your life."

He wasn't sure if he should believe her, but he lay still, and she began:

Many, many years ago, long before you or I were born, Cormundie was still one land. The mountains were but hills, and the rivers merely streams. Three brothers traveled down from the north – Demius, Domas, and Dolias. They found a golden desert and clear waters.

Demius was the oldest, and he made the decision to make this land their own. Domas was the strongest, and he kept away the sand leviathans so they could live in peace. The brothers bickered, but the lands continued to prosper.

107

It grew into a kingdom, but a kingdom needs a King, and the eldest brothers each thought they should rule. Both had friends and allies to become soldiers, and soon, it was a civil war.

The youngest brother Dolias begged for peace. He cried for them to love one another and rule together, but the elder two refused.

It ended in a violent battle on the land we're on now. The clashing of weapons and battle cries caused the sand leviathans to wake in a fury, and they split the sand and dirt, where the streams ballooned to rivers.

But the water ran red with blood.

When it was over, all the soldiers and both of the elder brothers had been killed.

Dolias and the others who had abstained from the war were the only survivors, and they went onto build the kingdom in the despair that came from losing everyone they had loved.

That is how Desperationis came to be. Dolias was the first King, and he named the rivers after the brothers he lost.

"Your mother used to tell you that story at bedtime?" Indy asked dubiously when she finished.

"She did always like dark fairy tales," Tris said with a crooked smile. "Now close your eyes and go to sleep."

He did as he was told, and instantly, he fell into the deepest, darkest sleep of his entire life.

He woke to the sound of flapping wings, and he opened his eyes to a pink morning sky. Around him, leaves were falling upward, from the ground beside him back up to the branches of the willow.

"Indy," Tris said, and he heard the urgency in her voice. "It's time for us to go."

He bolted up to see a pride of leoles – the winged lions – coming in to drink at the nearby river.

Tris was rolling up her blanket, and the horse and unicorn were stomping their feet and chuffing. Addonexus seemed particularly afraid of the leoles, and Indy rushed over to calm the animal before he ran off in terror.

The leoles didn't seem too concerned about them, but they were massive beasts, nearly as large as a horse. Majestic, feathered wings that matched the golden color of their fur grew from their backs. The males were even larger, with thick manes and ferocious teeth.

Leoles were not known for attacking humans, but with the Altering, Indy didn't want to take any chances. He rolled up his blanket and saddled up Addonexus and Velox, while Tris put out the fire.

Most of the leoles lapped up the river, but one of the males was watching Addonexus and Velox. His eyes never strayed as he stalked even closer to their campsite.

Indy and Tris hopped on their steeds, and they raced off into the desert with the sounds of big cats roaring and flapping wings behind them.

CHAPTER EIGHTEEN

THE MORSENEA DESERT WAS A LAND of bronze and black sand dunes, and little else to see for miles. Only sand and more sand, with an occasional gnarled plant or dried animal skeleton.

The glimmers of life that Tris did see were never pleasant. Vultures languidly flying in reverse circles, or the dunes moving like waves as the sand leviathan swam through them like an eel through water.

The ground rumbled, and the spines of the leviathan's back rippled through the sand. Tris spurred Velox on, but the horse had been running at top speed ever since the ground began to shake.

Suddenly, sand sprayed up before her as a leviathan erupted from the earth. Velox stopped short and reared back. Tris went flying off, landing on the hot ground.

The wind was knocked from her, and for a moment, she could only blink up at the blinding sun. A shadow fell over her, and the sand leviathan came into view. It was a copper-colored monstrosity with a mouth of jagged teeth, and it was large enough that it could swallow a horse whole.

Velox had run out of danger, and the eyeless leviathan was set on Tris. Slender tentacles surrounded the monster's gaping mouth. They probed and smelled, sensing the world around them, moving like inquisitive, ravenous serpents.

111

One of the tentacles touched Tris's ankle, and she tried to scramble back. The sand slipped underneath her, she couldn't get traction, and the hot, fetid breath of the leviathan overwhelmed her when it let out a hungry bellow.

"Get back!" Indy shouted as a gust of wind came up, blowing a whirlwind of sand right into the open mouth of the beast.

Tris was too afraid to take her eyes off the leviathan, but she heard Indy behind her. He grabbed her by the arm, yanking her to her feet, and then they were both running backward, away from the monster.

Indy kept the wind moving, with the sand disorienting the leviathan as it swirled around. The beast finally let out an annoyed cry before plummeting back underground.

"Thank you," Tris said breathlessly as they watched the sand rumbling away from them.

"You can thank me when we get to the city," Indy said. "But now, we need to get out of this desert as fast as we can."

Velox and Addonexus were waiting at a safe distance, and Tris and Indy hurriedly got on them. The animals raced faster after that, maybe realizing what they were running from. Minor creatures tended to steer clear of peccati, but the greatest beasts like the sand leviathans weren't so easily frightened.

By late afternoon, the waves of sand gave way to greener lands, with palm trees and tropical grass springing up.

Tris pushed the horse up the final hill that blocked her view of the capital city. The dry sandy earth slipped beneath the horse's hooves. The high winds and heavy rains of the recent procello had clearly caused some kind of landslide, and the mud and sand weren't the steady terrain they had been when Tris had left.

"Come on," Tris pushed Velox.

"The ground is too unsteady here," Indy called after her. "The animals can't go as fast up this hill."

Velox neighed in protest, and Tris eased up. She glanced back and saw that Indy was much further down the hill, with the larger unicorn struggling to make the trek.

Tris jumped down from Velox. The horse could move easier without her weighing him down, and she'd go faster on her own. Her feet slipped, and she had to half-walk half-crawl on all fours.

Breathless as she reached the crest, Tris finally looked down upon the capital city of Desperationis.

It was still standing. Trees were down, roofs were missing here and there, but from her vantage point, most of the homes and buildings were still there. The palace loomed tall and unchanged.

But the seaport and her home were still too far for her to see.

The horse and unicorn had made it up the unsteady ground, and from there, it was mostly dirt roads and occasional cobblestone, much easier for the animals to manage.

Tris and Indy climbed back on their respective steeds, and they rode down into the city. They hurried through the winding outer streets, where there were only minimal signs of damage. A missing shutter here, an upended tree there.

As they made it closer to the seaport, the destruction became more substantial. The glimpses she saw of Little Faunton as she passed by were distressing. Many of their structures appeared to have been swept out to sea, with only a few makeshift tents and half-collapsed buildings left.

Tris wanted to see if her own home was standing, so she didn't stop. Once she knew Reni was all right, she vowed to come back and help out the fauns.

Finally, she made it to the seaside, and she could see the little house on the rock. She dismounted Velox and left him on the mainland, so he wouldn't have to traverse the rickety bridge. As she ran across it, calling Reni's name, she noticed boards missing, and clumps of seaweed and debris stuck to the house when she reached it.

Inside wasn't quite as bad as Tris feared. Admittedly, everything she could see had been damaged. All the furniture and cabinets were waterlogged, and several of the chairs were missing. But the place had been straightened and cleaned. A chair was at the dining table, and blankets and clothing were hung across a line to dry.

A large section of the roof was missing over the main living area, and the back wall and bay window were gone entirely. Broken boards created a jagged frame to the sea crashing against the rock just beyond the opening.

"Reni?" Tris called again as she checked the back bedrooms. Both of them appeared largely intact, but Reni wasn't there. "Reni, where are you?"

"Maybe she went somewhere else to stay," Indy suggested.

He was behind her, tentatively picking up a blanket that had fallen off the clothesline when Tris rushed through.

"Reni would never leave this house for long, not when it's exposed like this," Tris said. The house had been in Reni's family for years. She would never abandon it or leave it to ruin.

Then Tris heard it – a gentle song carried through the opening in the wall, mixing with the wind and sea spray.

"Tris, come find me," she sang.

Indy had been standing in the middle of the room, but he turned to the sea with a faraway look. "What is that enchanting sound?"

But Tris didn't answer. She ran out through the wall onto the rocky island that held them, and she peered over the edge at the crashing waves.

Reni was treading water, her dark hair swirling around her as she grinned up at Tris. Shimmering green scales were sprinkled on her tawny skin, and from the waist down, she was all fish.

Tris knelt down on the edge of the rock. "Reni, what's happened? The moon isn't full. You aren't supposed to be a mermaid yet."

"Since the procello, I've been changing at will," Reni said. "I was tossed out of the house during the worst of it, and I awoke in the waves with my tail."

Reni grabbed onto the rocks and heaved herself up. Tris took her arm, helping her, and Reni sat beside her, with her glittering tail draped over the edge.

"Your roommate is a mermaid?" Indy asked in amazement, and both Tris and Reni looked back to see him standing in the opening in the wall.

"Weremer, actually," Reni corrected him. "I usually only transform under the full moon."

"The Altering is changing everything," Tris said.

Reni's tail started shifting. Tris had witnessed it many times over the years they'd lived together, but it was still a magical thing to see. The slick scales morphing into soft skin, and her singular tail split into two legs.

The transformation left Reni naked from the waist down, with only a wet blouse clinging to her body, barely hiding anything.

Indy cleared his throat and turned away, heading deeper into the house to give the half-naked Reni privacy.

Reni leaned over and whispered to Tris, "Who is your handsome friend?"

"Indy."

Reni's eyebrows arched sharply. "*Industria?*"

"He heard about the storm, and he wanted to help. That's why we rushed here."

"Well, we need all the help we can get," Reni said.

She got up and went into the house, and Tris followed behind her. Indy kept his back to them until Reni grabbed pants from the makeshift clothesline and pulled them on.

Once she was dressed, Reni told them about the procello. The hole in the wall seemed the most pressing issue, so that's where they got to work. Using broken wood and damaged boards that washed up on their rocky island, they began patching it up.

Tris had only just swung a hammer when someone knocked at the door. She opened it, and there was Ira, scowling at her under his mop of fiery red hair.

"The King heard you were back in town, and he wants to see you," Ira said. "*Now.*"

CHAPTER NINETEEN

TRIS TRIED TO KEEP UP WITH IRA as they walked through the city, but he kept speeding up. No matter how fast she walked, he insisted on being a step or two in front of her.

It had not been that long ago that she was showing Ira around, now he acted like he was leading her. But she was too exhausted and stressed to bother with Ira's petty games.

The Emerald Palace stood intact and without any obvious signs of damage, other than broken vines and patchy moss. Since it was carved into stone, it weathered most anything thrown at it.

It was quiet inside the palace when it was usually bustling with guards and servants. Tris saw hardly anyone, just a sniveling sonneillon and a human guard. Then she realized she hadn't seen any fauns anywhere near the palace, when many of them worked here as servants.

Tris and Ira were nearly to the throne room when he finally broke the tense silence. "You aren't even going to ask how I fared?"

"I… You've been staying at the palace," she stammered, caught off guard by his accusatory tone. "I assumed you were fine."

He snorted derisively. "Of course. You're off gallivanting across Cormundie to get fancy honey.

Your kingdom has been hit by a major procello, and you assume we're all *fine*."

"I only just got in," she argued.

He stopped and glared at her. "It has been really hard while you were gone. The King doesn't want to do anything, I don't know what I even can do, Sabina is overwhelmed...." He exhaled roughly. "We needed you, and you weren't here."

"I... I'm sorry," Tris said at length. "I won't abandon you or the kingdom like that again."

She couldn't tell if Ira believed her or not, but he just turned and went on to the throne room.

King Dolorin was lounging on his throne made of carved leviathan bones. The spot next to him where Sabina usually stood was conspicuously empty, although Mephis the sonneillon was at his right hand. He had taken on Tris's role as consiliarius while she was on her errand.

"Where is my honey?" the King demanded.

"As soon as I heard of the procello, I turned around and returned to the kingdom," Tris said. "I hadn't had a chance yet to procure your ambrosian honey."

He rolled his eyes and let out an exasperated sigh. "Of course you didn't, and you haven't been to see me."

"I only just returned," Tris explained. "I went to my home first to see if it was still standing."

"Was it?" he asked darkly.

"For the most part, yes."

"That's better than many," the King said, but he sounded bored by the very idea. "There is much to rebuild and limited stockpiles.

"Some of the nobility and gentry have homes that were damaged," he went on. "Their repairs should be

118

the priority, and I need you to ensure they are comfortable until then."

Hospitality endeavors were the most tedious part of her job, and since Sabina had been working as the seneschal, it had fallen into the faun's purview.

"Has Sabina been handling that in my absence?" Tris asked.

King Dolorin shook his head wildly, like a petulant child. "She's been busy with other things, too busy to do her job."

"I did see that Little Faunton had nearly been swept out to the sea," Tris said.

Dolorin snapped his harsh gaze at her, instantly outraged. "You visited the slums of the fauns before you visited me, your Master?"

"Valefor is our Master," Ira corrected him, and the King seethed at them both.

"And where is he?" the King bellowed. "Lost somewhere in the clouds? I am here, the ruler of the prosperous seaport kingdom, King of the Vespertine Sea and the Morsenea Desert. I am the one you answer to when Valefor is absent!"

"Of course, Sire," Tris said, bowing her head before him as not to further incur his wrath. "We are happy to serve you."

"Then why is nobody serving me?" Dolorin demanded, practically whining. "All of the fauns who are supposed to be here in the palace working are wallowing in their squalor instead."

There was hardly any point in explaining to him that many of the fauns were injured or killed, and their homes and families were quite literally destroyed. They hadn't shown up to work because many of them were physically incapable of it or they were holding together what little they had left of their lives.

But Dolorin would neither hear nor understand that. He was King, and his every want took precedent over his kingdom's needs, even in times of crisis. Perhaps *especially* in times of crisis.

"The procello only just happened," Tris gently reminded the King.

"With Tris back, she and I can continue with Sabina's duties until she's able to —" Ira began before the King interrupted.

"Sabina should have returned today!" he shouted, and from the corner of her eye, Tris noticed Ira flinch.

"Why do you not propose an edict?" Mephis suggested. He stood beside the throne, sneering and toying with the glimmering irin-bone dagger sheathed on his belt. "Your word is law. If you commanded everyone to work, then they must work."

"Your people are barely surviving," Tris argued evenly, and she chose her words careful and deliberate. "They will be of no use to you if those working are half-dead. Give them five more days, then pronounce the edict. Until then, Ira and I can manage."

Dolorin exhaled heavily and toyed with the rings on his hand. "If you truly think that you and Ira can handle all my business... then so be it. You have *two* days. Then everyone who has not returned to work will be rounded up and thrown into the dungeon."

"Yes, of course, Your Majesty," Tris said.

The King rattled off a list of tasks that she and Ira needed to ensure were completed. It was quite extensive, and she was growing weary just listening to it.

Finally, Dolorin dismissed them, and Tris went toward her chancery. This time, Ira slowed so he was in step beside her.

"Why did you try to stop his edict?" he asked her.

"We can't have all the servants in the dungeon," she said. "Nothing will get done. I'm willing to do Sabina's work for a few days if it means I won't have to do it forever."

"So... you're lazy, not sympathetic?" he questioned.

She kept her eyes straight ahead so he wouldn't see the truth when she said, "Right. I don't care about anything other than my own workload."

"But... our duty is to spread suffering," Ira persisted, but he sounded confused and conflicted, as opposed to accusatory. "You're alleviating it for your own benefit."

"Everything I do is for my own benefit, Ira," Tris snapped in exasperation, and she turned to face him. "I'm a peccati. We're all selfish assholes. You should already know that by now."

She turned and stalked off to her chancery, but Ira didn't follow. She had much work to do, and she had to find a way to warn Sabina and the other fauns about what was to come.

121

CHAPTER TWENTY

INDY SPENT THE EVENING HELPING RENI patch up her little house. He was happy to help, but as the night went on, his worry began to grow.

When that wiry little peccati had shown up, Indy tried to think of a way to prevent him from taking Tris. He had known it was Ira just by the looks of him. His anger hung on him like a shroud, and even his scowl had a sharp edge to it.

But Indy couldn't do anything. Tris worked for King Dolorin, a ruler who had been under Valefor's thumb since before he was born. If the King were to discover that a virtu was helping Tris, it wouldn't go well for either Tris or Indy.

Dolorin might not recognize him as the Industria – it wasn't as obvious to humans – but Ira would see it, the way Indy had seen it on him.

So, Indy had stayed hidden behind the broken wall, peering through a crack between the boards. He watched Tris leave with a dangerous man, and he had to trust that she could handle herself. She was a peccati, after all.

Not that he was even sure what that meant anymore. In the time he'd spent with Tris, she was kind, driven, and loyal, all things he had never thought possible of someone like her.

How could that be? And what did that say about him and the other virtus? If the peccati aren't all bad, then were virtus truly all good?

Those weren't his most pressing worries, however. The waning moon was high in the sky, his body ached from the day's work, and Tris still hadn't returned.

Indy stood at the window that faced the mainland, staring at the bridge that crossed the sea. Behind him, Reni was doing some last-minute tidying before she went to her bedroom for the night.

"You shouldn't wait up for her," Reni said.

He looked back over his shoulder and realized that Reni had been setting up a sleeping area for him. A hammock in the corner with blankets. "You didn't need to go through all that trouble."

"It's no trouble. You helped me plenty today." Reni smiled up at him. "But you should rest. When the King is in a foul mood, he keeps her working until dawn."

He frowned. "Working doing what?"

She shrugged. "Whatever tedious nonsense he puts her through."

"And she doesn't mind that?"

Reni laughed, and the beads and braids in her long wavy hair swayed. "Of course she does. She minds plenty, but it's her duty. She does what she's commanded to do. Same as you, I suppose."

He looked away from her then, letting his gaze go to the moon, shining in through the hole in the roof they hadn't yet repaired.

"Is that why you're here?" Reni asked quietly. "Because your Mistress sent you?"

"No, she doesn't know I'm here," he admitted. "I'm meant to be watching over a virtu."

"Why are you here?" she asked, then quickly added, "Not that I'm complaining."

"I like to help those in need," Indy said, but that wasn't the entire truth.

Tris had been devastated when she'd heard about what happened to her home. Her face blanched, her eyes wide and horrified. He wanted to help her. He wanted to comfort her and take away her pain and sadness.

That had been enough for him to leave his duties and follow Tris through the wilds of Cormundie, unmindful of the dangers because he was by her side.

"Doesn't it go against your vows to help us?" Reni asked. "Desperationis is renowned for our unsavory characters. The King is a despot, the nobles are cruel profiteers. Even I spend months at sea, making a living as a pirate."

He offered her a crooked smile. "I help those who need it, not only those who live an unblemished life."

"Does anyone really live an unblemished life?" she wondered aloud.

"No," he said softly, quiet enough that she didn't hear him.

Reni yawned and stretched. "I'm off to bed before I fall asleep on my feet." As she turned and headed back to her room, she called, "Don't stay up too late."

Indy looked over at the little area she'd set up for him, and he wished he could take Reni's advice. But he knew sleep wouldn't come for him, especially not when Tris was still out there, working for a spiteful King.

He didn't want to wake Reni with his agitated pacing, so he slipped out into the night to walk the city alone.

On the mainland, near the bridge that connected Tris and Reni's house, was a small stable that managed to survive the storm. For a few coin, Velox and Addonexus were housed there, and Indy stopped by to check on them. The animals seemed to be doing well, enjoying their rest after the long journey across Cormundie.

After that, Indy moved on, wandering the darkened streets. Many of the gas lanterns that would've brightened the city were broken or swept away, and several of the ones that had been left, no one had bothered to light them.

That was until he grew closer to Little Faunton. He could see glimpses of the warm glow and heard cheery music playing on a pan flute. He rounded a bend, and finally, he could see them. Dozens of fauns working together through the night to continue rebuilding their neighborhood.

The strong were building walls, chopping wood, while the elderly and children wove reeds for roofs or mended fabric for clothes and blankets. Others worked a cauldron over a firepit, keeping a fragrant stew going so everyone could eat.

There working among the fauns, Indy spied Tris. She'd discarded her jacket, so she worked in her corseted vest and white blouse with the sleeves pushed up. Her dark hair was pulled up from her face, and she wiped at the smudge of dirt on her brow.

When she noticed him watching, she smiled, and he swore he'd never seen anything more enchanting.

She wiped her hands on her trousers as she made her way over to him. "What are you doing out here?"

"Couldn't sleep," he said, glancing around. "Is this what your King has you doing?"

"Not exactly." She turned sheepish and lowered her gaze. "He's only allowing the fauns another two days to rebuild, so I'm helping them get as much done as they can."

"Tris has been working tirelessly," a faun interjected. She had come up beside them, her nose twitching subtly like a rabbit. "She even got Ira to pitch in for a time, but he left to sleep a while ago."

"Sabina is once again singing my praises too much," Tris demurred. "I have only done what needs to be done. Nothing more."

"Just because you are Tristitia does not mean you can't show pride in the work you do," Sabina said.

"Are you planning to rest before the sun rises?" Indy asked Tris.

"If there is time," she said wearily.

"Tris, please, do not work yourself to death," Sabina said. "I need you to help me handle the King."

"Why don't we head back home?" Indy suggested. "In the morning, I can return to help them here. I'll work twice as hard to make up for the time you're sleeping."

She cast him a wry look. "I'll hold you to it."

Tris grabbed her jacket and promised Sabina and the other fauns she'd return to help as soon as she was able. Once she bid them farewell, Indy and Tris walked slowly through the crumbling city, neither of them saying much.

The silence felt nice, though. As they walked back toward the seashore, a mist settled over them. There was something so peaceful and intimate about the two of them, alone together, and he slowly felt the tension and fear of the day loosening in his muscles. They'd been knotted in his shoulders, clenching in his stomach, aching in his chest.

By the time they'd returned to Tris's house, Indy felt lighter and calmer, just by being in her presence.

When she went inside, she let out an approving whistle – quiet, as not to wake Reni, but clearly impressed. She admired the work they'd done. Her fingers running across the boards he'd carefully nailed up, roughly repairing the wall.

"You do good work, Indy. I'll have to enlist you more often."

"And I'd be happy to oblige."

She smiled at him over her shoulder, her green eyes sparkling, and his heart leapt in his chest.

But it was more than a leap, more than a quickening of desire. This was a *pull*. A longing so intense and so certain, he could hardly keep his feet in place.

Indy somehow managed to keep from running to her, but he couldn't take his eyes off her, not when she smiled at him like that.

She looked away first, taking in the rest of the work he and Reni had done in the room, but her gaze stopped when it landed on the hammock.

"We both deserve to put our feet up after the day we've had." She bent over to unbuckle her calf-high boots, and Indy decided to do the same.

When she was finished, she walked barefoot across the room to grab a pitcher of sun tea from off the table. She went back to the hammock and lounged in it with her legs hanging over the edge.

"Well?" Tris motioned to the empty spot beside her. "Are you going to join me or not?"

With less than a moment of hesitation, he went over to her. He climbed into the hammock as gracefully as he could. Tris had made maneuvering in the taut netting seem easier than it was, but he managed to do it without hurting her or himself.

There was no way to put distance between them, even if he wanted to, and he didn't. They were sitting hip to hip, their shoulders touching, as they looked up at the sliver of moon and swirling stars above them.

He was closer to her now than he'd ever been, but still, his heart told him they were not close enough. Through the fabric that separated them, he could feel the heat of her, and the softness of her body.

Tris held up the pitcher of sun tea. "Cheers to our surprising new friendship!" She took a swig, then held the pitcher out to him.

He took it, his cool fingers brushing against hers. "Cheers."

"I haven't really known any virtus in my life," she said, watching him as he drank. "But you're not as I expected. Or, really, at first you were *exactly* as I expected, but then I realized that there was more."

He eyed her curiously. "How did I seem at first?"

"Oh, you know. Uptight, judgmental, humorless."

It stung hearing her describe him that way, even though he'd heard it all before. Many years ago, he'd had a paramour who called him "utterly joyless" before leaving him.

Yet, it hurt even worse than that to know Tris felt the same way.

"But you're not. Or maybe you are, but you're not *only* those things," she amended gently. "You are kind and selfless, and if you have hard edges, it's only because you must be strong in a world that is so often cruel."

His voice was thick when he said, "Thank you. I worry that… most people don't see me." He braved looking over at her, smiling up at him in the moonlight.

Tris put her hand on his face, her thumb hot on his cheek, and her fingers in his beard. "The more I see of you, the more I know of you… the more I grow to care for you."

He wanted to say that he felt the same way about her, that he found her to be so compassionate and kind and beautiful… but he couldn't fight the pull any longer.

He leaned over and his lips found hers. He dropped the pitcher so he could pull her into his arms and kiss her fiercely.

CHAPTER TWENTY-ONE

TRIS HAD BEEN KISSED many times before, but this was the first time a kiss truly took her breath away. Her eyes were closed, but she was certain if she opened them, she'd see that both her and Indy were glowing from within.

She could *feel* the glow. Tingling and hot as it radiated through her skin.

And then she breathed him in – sea salt and sweet tea and fresh cut lumber. Her heart raced into life, with each and every beat thrumming in delight.

She kissed him deeply, their tongues entwined, and she gripped onto him. Her body, her very being wanted him with a desire more than want, more than need.

They moved together roughly, quickly, in a frenzy of lust, and that didn't mix well with the hammock. They tumbled out of it together and fell onto the floor.

Indy managed to slide himself under her, catching her and shielding her from the fall. She knew she shouldn't be surprised, but she was anyway, because she could never trust anyone to catch her before.

She trusted him already, and that should terrify her, but instead she felt safe and happy.

Within moments, they had stripped each other of their clothes, and they found their way together, uniting their bodies in glorious, sweaty, happiness.

They lay on the floor together, tangled up in blankets and each other. Her head was on his chest, listening to his heart beating in time with hers, and he stroked her back as they stared up at the sky.

"I hope we didn't wake your friend," Indy said softly.

"Reni sleeps like the dead," she assured him.

"Can... can I ask you something?"

She tilted her head up to get a look at him. "You can ask me anything."

"How did you end up as the Tristitia?"

She sighed and relaxed into his arms again. "It's not a very exciting story, I'm afraid. But I'll tell you anyway.

"I grew up not too far from here," she went on. "It was nothing but a blip of a village, outside the capital on the edge of the Morsenea Desert, before the ground gave way completely to the sand. I had a mother and father, a younger sister and two brothers. We had a few friends, and we raised lanalepus."

Lanalepus were small woolly hares with curled horns like a ram. They were cute, docile, and consumed very little water, so they made good livestock for desert folk. Tris and her family raised them for their wool, which they sheared several times a year.

"I was the oldest child, so my father sent me to the capital to sell our lanalepus wool," she said. "And when I came back..."

She closed her eyes, and she could still see what she'd found when she returned. Their homes destroyed, every living thing missing. She ran through the shambles of her village, screaming for her family.

Then the sand had rumbled. The earth quaked beneath her feet, and she heard the maw of the ground opening. The sand leviathan surfaced mere feet from her. The tentacles were outstretched, sensing the air.

Tris had yelled and hurled a rock, demanding the beast eat her too. But the leviathan had eaten its fill. It slid off slowly through the dunes, to digest its meal in the sun, and she had been left alone, with nothing.

"... everyone was gone," she finished at length. "A sand leviathan had gotten them all."

Indy's arm tightened around her. "I am so sorry."

"It was a long, long time ago." She brushed off his apology and blinked her tears back before they fell. "I went into a deep despair afterwards, and I sat in the wreckage of my life and waited for death.

"But instead, Valefor found me," she continued. "I don't know how or why, and I was too despondent to even ask him. He promised me a way out of the pain, and I would've done anything to be free of it.

"So I went with him, and I pledged myself to him," she said with a rough exhale. "I gained a few things in exchange – immortality, conjuring fire, putting others to sleep – but he never did take away the pain. He couldn't, of course, he'd merely lied."

Indy held her close and kissed her hair. "I am happy that you're Tris, because you are amazing. But I am very sorry that you went through all that pain and that you went through it alone."

She kissed his chest and let him comfort her, but she wouldn't let the tears fall.

"What did your parents name you?" he asked.

"Viridiana. But she died a long time ago. She was a sixteen-year-old human girl with foolish dreams and silly thoughts, and... she's gone, and I've been Tristitia ever since. I *am* Tris."

She snuggled closer to him, pressing her skin against his cool flesh. "I don't want to think of any of that anymore. This moment is not meant for the darkness of the past."

"I might have something that will take your mind off that," Indy said, sounding sheepish.

She half-expected him to kiss her, but instead, he took a deep breath, and he lifted his hand that wasn't on her. He twisted his fingers in the air, and she felt a soft breeze swirl through the room. It smelled of the sea and tasted sweet.

In the moonlight, the glittery bits of dust and sand gathered with a wispy white smoke above where they laid. Slowly, as Indy moved his finger, the glittering smoke took form.

A man and woman dancing together. It grew more detailed until it was as clear as any sketch or painting, and Tris gasped when she realized it was *them*. Her and Indy, the night they'd danced together at Lux and Lily's wedding.

Rendered in the smoke, Tris appeared far more beautiful than she had ever been. Indy had reproduced her in exquisite detail. The glittering dust even captured the emerald green of her gown.

"You've made me look so magnificent," she said in an awed whisper.

"You *are* magnificent," he told her firmly.

She moved, propping herself up on her elbow so she could look him in the eye when she asked, "Is that really how you saw me? Even when we first met?"

"Yes," he said thickly. "I thought you were magnificent and terrifying, and I knew I wanted to know you."

She tilted her head, trying to absorb his words. "Can you lie?"

He smirked. "I can, but I'm not now."

"But you can sin?" she pressed.

134

"I'm as capable of cruelty as much as you are of kindness."

She narrowed her eyes slightly. "We are both capable of quite a lot then."

"But I choose kindness. I choose whatever it is to be with you."

"What do you suppose us being together is? Good or bad? Am I corrupting you, or are you saving me?"

"Why can't we save each other?" he asked simply.

Tris kissed him then, because she desperately wanted that to be true. She ran her fingers through his thick hair and looked him in his stony gray eyes.

"I want to stay up all night kissing you and talking with you, but I fear I am much too tired," she admitted.

"Don't let me keep you awake just because I can't sleep," Indy said.

"Do you want me to help?" She caressed his forehead. "You've certainly earned a good night's rest."

He hesitated. She could see the fatigue darkening his eyes, and he bit his lip.

"Why are you reluctant to accept my help?" she asked softly. "Why, when you so clearly need it?"

He licked his lips and stared off into the night. "I am as my Mistress intends me to be. The sleep I get is the sleep I deserve, or why else would she make it so?"

"For a thousand reasons, honestly, Indy." Tris was aghast. "If your Mistress is good and kind, she wouldn't want you to suffer. It's my Master who is meant to hand out pain. Insomnia is an ailment to be treated, not a punishment to be served."

She stroked his cheek, so he'd look her in the eyes again, and she smiled sadly down at him. "You deserve rest and happiness as much as anyone else."

He smiled at her, and when she traced her thumb along his bottom lip, he kissed it. "Okay. Put me to sleep, Tris."

She ran her fingers down his temples, and his eyes fluttered close. He breathed deep and slow as he drifted off to sleep.

"You poor boy, so tired all the time with the weight of the world on your shoulders," she whispered. "Good night." She kissed his forehead and curled up beside him.

Within moments, she was lost in a dark and dreamless sleep.

CHAPTER TWENTY-TWO

TRIS AWOKE IN THE MORNING, cold and alone on the floor. The birds perched on the roof were letting out their warbled inverse song the way they had since the Altering began. Over the birds, she heard the whistle of the kettle, and the earthy scent of tea filled the house.

Holding the blanket to her chest, she sat up and looked around. Indy was dressed in his shirt and pants with his back to her, standing at the stove.

"Do you want any tea?" he asked without looking at her, as if he had sensed she was awake.

"Yes, please," she said and hurriedly pulled on her clothes before he turned around. In the bright light of morning, she had no idea how she felt about bedding a virtu.

He brought her a cup, and then they stood across from each other, each sipping their hot drink and waiting in an awkward silence.

"Have you been awake long?" she asked.

He averted his gaze. "Not too long." He took another drink, then said, "About last night —"

Before he could say anything more, the front door opened. Reni walked inside, her nightgown and hair dripping wet, and a slippery moray eel was on a hook, slung over her shoulder.

"Good morning, sleepyheads," Reni said cheerily and grinned at the two of them. "I went out to catch something to eat for the day."

"Morning," Tris said as Reni put the moray in the ice chest to store until she cooked it up later.

"Good morning, Reni," Indy said, sounding stilted and formal. "I made tea."

"Great, but is there enough for a couple more?" she asked.

Tris looked to her in confusion. "What? Why?"

"You've got a couple guests coming up the bridge. Fancy ones by the looks of it." Reni pointed to the window that faced the mainland.

"*What*?" Tris repeated. Both she and Indy rushed over to the window to see a gilded carriage waiting on the shore, and Lux and Lily were walking up the bridge to the house.

"I'm going to put on something dry," Reni said before disappearing back into her bedroom.

"Did you summon them?" Indy asked Tris but his eyes were locked on the upcoming newlyweds.

Tris prickled. "No. How could I have? And why? It's dangerous for them here, especially with King Dolorin's mood."

"Lily said they'd send aid, but I didn't think she would come here herself," Indy grumbled in frustration.

He pulled on his belt and boots, and Tris stayed at the window, wondering how to deal with the likelihood that everyone in the city had already noticed the ostentatious guests rolling through.

Which meant that Dolorin and Ira would soon know traitors were in Desperationis, and that Tris was colluding with them.

As soon as Indy had his boots on – still unfastened because he apparently didn't want to waste time – he opened the front door. With a tight smile, he motioned them onward. "Lily, Lux, hurry inside so we can talk."

Lux picked up his pace, but Lily let go of his hand and sprinted ahead. She threw her arms around Indy, hugging him tightly, and Indy's smile only grew more pained as he greeted her.

"We were so worried about you and everyone here," Lily said. "We couldn't enjoy our honeymoon when we knew you were suffering."

"The sentiment is appreciated," Indy told her carefully. "But you needn't rush out here, especially not in such a gawdy craft."

"What do you mean?" Lux asked as Indy shut the door behind them.

"You came into Desperationis like a peacock, and everyone likely noticed," Tris said flatly. "That's a bold move when King Dolorin and Valefor aren't friendly with Insontia."

"We thought this would ease the tensions, if we offered a hand," Lily said.

Indy rubbed his temple and sighed. "You can't just visit a hostile kingdom when you're the princess of enemy lands."

"I am trying to rule in a kinder way." Lily lifted her chin indignantly, and Lux slipped a supportive arm around her waist. "With Valefor exiled, we seek to unite Cormundie."

"He may be gone, but his minions aren't," Tris reminded them. "Ira and the sonneillons are in King Dolorin's ear, enacting Valefor's wishes. And the thing Valefor wants the most right now is to wipe the two of you off the world."

Lily had gone pale and lowered her eyes.

"We only meant to help," Lux insisted.

"Why didn't your father try to stop you?" Indy asked Lily. "Or Wick? Or Aeterna?"

"They don't know that we're here," she admitted quietly. "We were vacationing in a chateau in Insontia, but we decided to leave early and come here instead."

"You truly are a sheltered princess," Indy muttered under his breath. Louder, to Tris, he said, "We need to hide the carriage and keep Lux and Lily hidden."

"There's no need for any of that," Lily said. "If we're going to be trouble, we can just turn around and go."

"And have that carriage pass through the city again when everyone is heading out for the day?" Indy shook his head. "No, we need to hide it, and you'll have to wait until after dark to leave."

Reni came out of the bedroom in dry clothes with a bandana wrapped around her head, holding back her damp hair. "So, Tris, who are your new friends?"

Tris made quick introductions. "This is the Castimonia, but she goes by Lily, and her husband, Luxuria."

"Maxon," Lux corrected her. "I'm using my birth name now, since I'm not really the Luxuria."

"Maxon, then," Tris said and looked back at her roommate. "This is Reni."

"I'm Tris's roommate, closest friend, and I'm a weremer with a heart of gold." Reni grinned at them as she shook their hands. "I also know a thing or two about smuggling and hiding valuables."

"You know somewhere we could conceal that glittering carriage outside?" Indy asked.

Reni nodded. "Anything smaller than an elephant, I can hide."

Indy crouched down to finish fastening his boots. "Let's go get this eyesore out of the way." He looked up at Tris. "You stay back here and keep them out of sight." After he finished, he straightened up. "When I get back, we'll figure out how to handle this."

Tris wanted to protest. She didn't much like hosting guests, especially unexpected ones. But Indy seemed fixated on the carriage, so she'd let him deal with that. Besides, he and Reni were practically out the door the moment they were ready.

"Sorry about all of this," Lux – *Maxon* said, and he sat back on a barrel, using it like a chair. "I'm obviously not well-versed with the whole 'doing good,' and my intentions were never to be an imposition."

Lily walked over to her husband, gently rubbing his shoulder. "Luminelle told me that Cormundie needs to be united, and that's all I've been trying to do."

"That is admirable," Tris said. "But since you're both new to this, maybe you should check with Indy or your King or your Mistress before making major decisions."

Lily frowned, and Lux put an arm around her and pulled her onto his lap. "It is true that I haven't had much practice in ruling a kingdom, and I have been so busy training with Indy and planning the wedding. But I've been thrust into this, with my father an aging and passive King."

"Fortunately for you, I have been advising Kings for a very long time," Tris said. "I know very well about how to soothe an enraged monarch."

CHAPTER TWENTY-THREE

THIS HADN'T BEEN HOW LILY WANTED this to go.
Hiding out in the dilapidated house of a peccati she
barely knew and that she didn't fully trust. Outside,
the waves were thrashing against the rocks, and sea
spray filtered in through the opening of the roof in a
fine mist.

All she wanted to do was finish the work of her
mother and follow the bidding of Luminelle. For too
many years, her father had been a complacent King,
letting Lily's stepmother do as she pleased with the
kingdom's coffer.

But her stepmother had disappeared before the
Altering, and Lily had left behind her isolated life to
truly become the Crown Princess. With Maxon at her
side, they could help who needed it, and bring peace
and harmony across the lands.

Now, in their first attempts to do so, they had
only brought danger to those they sought to help. Indy
had left in an anxious hurry to hide the carriage, and a
storm was brewing outside.

"I've made a terrible mess of things, haven't I?"
Lily asked, softly to herself as she stared up at the
sky.

"You've complicated things, but it's not a mess
yet," Tris said, her voice at her shoulder startling her.
Lily hadn't realized she was so close.

Tris gave her a smile that was likely meant to be reassuring, but to Lily, it only looked sickly. "Indy and I will take care of things."

Lily, Maxon, and Tris discussed what to do. To appease King Dolorin, Tris said they would have to offer something – wood to rebuild, crops for the townsfolk, some gold and riches to sweeten the deal. It was only a little more than what they had planned to give anyway, so Lily agreed easily.

Once Indy and Reni returned, Tris would leave to go see the King. She would pretend to have invited Maxon to make up for his "betrayal," and she would make a big show of all that they wanted to share with Desperationis.

"All of that should be enough to spare you," Tris said. "But you should be ready to make a quick escape if needed."

"We will do what we have to do to make this right," Lily promised.

"A quick escape?" Maxon asked, and his arm went protectively around his wife's waist again, the way he did whenever there was a hint of danger. "How can we do that if the carriage is hidden?"

"Your horses are still here," Tris reminded them. "They will ride much faster than a carriage anyway.

"Addonexus and Velox?" Lily said, brightening at the mention of the unicorn and horse. "How are they? Where are they? Did they make the journey okay?"

"They did wonderful, and they are resting in a nearby stable and getting extra helpings of fresh oats," Tris assured her.

With their plan set, Lily and Maxon didn't want to just wait around for the others to return.

They had left in the middle of the night because Lily couldn't sleep. She'd woken from a terrible nightmare, and she'd known all at once that she could not wallow in their splendor, removed from the troubles of Cormundie. So she'd woken Maxon and insisted they leave to help others, and they had.

Yet so far, she had only made things worse.

To counter that, she and Maxon went about helping Tris fix up her home while they waited. He had done some handywork over his time as the Luxuria, and he knew enough how to swing a hammer.

To close up the hole in the roof, Maxon and Tris had climbed up on top of the house. Lily stayed below to hand them tools and wood, and they had been working quite well until Tris suddenly groaned.

"Tris, what's the matter?" Maxon asked, and he barely caught her before she fell to the floor.

"I don't know." Tris grimaced, and she had one hand on her head, and the other went to her stomach. "I just… I have phantom pains all over."

"Maybe the work is getting to you?" Lily asked. "You should get down from the roof. It doesn't seem safe for you now."

Maxon took her arm and helped Tris down. She leaned against the wall, holding her stomach and frowning.

"It's just the strangest thing," Tris muttered. "The pains came out of nowhere."

Lily heard someone distantly calling Tris's name. Without saying anything, Tris hobbled over and opened the front door. That's when Lily realized that it was the weremer, Reni, calling for her.

"What's wrong?" Tris asked as Reni raced into the house with wild eyes. "Where's Indy?"

"They grabbed him," Reni said.

"Who? What are you talking about?" Tris demanded.

"The King's men. Some human soldiers and sonneillons."

Lily gasped, and her hand went to her mouth. Her stomach lurched at the thought of something happening to Indy. He'd become an older brother to her, and with him being so powerful and knowledgeable, he seemed indestructible.

But the King's men had overpowered and captured him. It was disorienting and horrifying to imagine, and guilt twisted her heart. If she hadn't come here, he wouldn't have been hiding her carriage.

Whatever befell Indy was because of her, and she had to find a way to make it right.

"Why?" Maxon asked. He'd gotten down from the roof and joined them all by the door. "Because of our carriage?"

Reni shook her head. "We hid it near Little Faunton, and the King's men were clearing the slums. Dolorin rounded up all the fauns and threw them in the dungeon."

"*No*," Tris said in disbelief. "Dolorin said he'd wait two days. It's too soon."

"They were capturing the last few fauns that escaped them," Reni explained in a frantic, desperate tone. "Indy tried to stop them, so they took him, too."

"Damn, damn, *damn*," Tris said and looked toward the Emerald Palace. "We're all damned now."

CHAPTER TWENTY-FOUR

THE SKY WAS DARKENING as the clouds rolled in, but it hadn't yet begun to rain when Tris walked toward the palace. The winds weren't even strong, but fish were littering the shore, motionless unless they were being picked at by the birds.

She slunk along on side streets and kept her head down to avoid the King's men marching down the narrow roads. The strange weather and armed soldiers stomping about kept most everyone indoors. This left the city eerily quiet, and she caught glimpses of townsfolk hiding in their homes still in disrepair.

Her pain had subsided to a dull throb, and she didn't let it slow her down. When Tris finally reached the palace, she found it sparsely guarded. Most of them were out arresting the fauns, and that left only an old pair of sonneillons watching the door.

She went to walk between them into the palace, the way she did every morning, but they lowered their pilum spears, crossing them to create an X that blocked her path.

"What is your business here?" one of them asked.

"I am Tristitia, the consiliarius to King Dolorin. I am here to advise the King."

The sonneillons exchanged a look with their narrow yellow eyes. Their peeling skin flaked off as they scratched their heads and considered her.

"He has not summoned you," he argued.

"Because I am already expected," Tris snapped. "Let me through."

"I shall check with the King first," the other said.

"I don't have time for this," she muttered.

Tris had worked in the palace for decades, and she knew every inch of it. Including the secret side entrances hidden by vines. They had been installed so the royalty could quickly make an escape in times of danger, but the doorways also worked well when she needed to sneak in or out.

She went along the side of the palace, feeling around the vines and pushing through overgrown ferns until she finally found the door. Then she slipped inside and jogged to the throne room. That's where Dolorin always was at this time of day, or most any time of day. He loved nothing more than sitting on his throne made of bones, presiding over everyone.

So it was her great surprise when she marched into the throne room and found his sacred chair empty. But then she heard his voice, softly echoing in the corridor that connected the room to his chambers, and the dim glow of firelight bounced off the walls.

"— are as guilty as anyone," the King was saying. "The fauns are takers and users, and they deserve no pity."

"But Sire —" That was Ira's voice, disagreeing with the King, but he stopped the moment he stepped out of the corridor and saw Tris.

He had been walking beside the King, with his hand held over his head. Ira was using his flaming fingertips like a lantern in the darkened passageway.

"Tristitia," King Dolorin greeted her wearily. Her anger must've been written on her face because he said, "You've heard about the edict."

"Why did you not wait the two days we discussed?" Tris demanded, barely keeping her voice even.

"Because I did not want to delay the inevitable," Dolorin said as he took his seat on the throne.

"But what about the work the fauns do? Who will do that now?" she countered.

Dolorin cast a look between them – Ira stood near Tris, both of them standing before him. "So he is your mouthpiece, or are you his, Tristitia? Because you're saying the same party line."

"We are in agreement with our Master's wishes," Tris contended.

"When were you last in contact with Valefor?" the King asked. "How long has it been since you last spoke with him?"

"I-I'm not sure," she faltered, because it had been some time. In general, she avoided talking to Valefor, and she hadn't connected with him since he had been banished.

"I spoke with him last night," the King said. "We talked through my cauldron, and he told me his utmost wish is for suffering and chaos to reign down on Cormundie. He supports any edict I propose as long as it causes misery and turmoil."

"Sire," Tris said carefully.

"And do you know what our Master told me?" Dolorin went on as if she'd said nothing. "That the other virtus are trying to sway you, the way the Castimonia worked on the weak and traitorous Luxuria."

She struggled to keep her expression neutral, swallowing back her growing unease, and she kept her mouth shut as the King continued his castigation.

"Of course, Valefor doesn't think that either you or Ira are as pathetic and weak as Lux," he said. "But he wanted us all to be on the lookout for predatory virtus."

The King rested his hand on his chin. His mouth was turned up in a satisfied smirk, and that never boded well for Tris.

"Valefor turned out to be very prescient with that," Dolorin continued. "No sooner had he warned me about scheming virtus, I found the Industria creeping in our midst, and I just received word that Luxuria and Castimonia arrived this morning."

Ira was standing right beside her, but the King's harsh gaze was locked only on Tris. She waited a beat, hoping he'd say more, but he was clearly waiting on her. Something had to be said, and she'd have to be the one to say it.

"Good that our Master warned you. He truly can see so much from his current realm."

"More than he could when he was here," King Dolorin agreed ominously.

"Have you arrested all the virtus then?" Tris asked, as if she didn't know, as if they weren't hiding in her house with Reni.

"Not yet," the King said with a sigh. "But I have eyes everywhere. As soon as all three of them are brought in, I will kill them in a grand fashion in the courtyard. Them, and a few of the faun dissenters."

A wave of nausea washed over Tris. The scent of blood filled her nostrils as she remembered the time the King's father had showed his force and brutality in the palace courtyard.

"Dissenters?" Ira asked.

"Yes, the leaders who pushed back. Sabina and the like," he said with a dismissive wave of his hand.

"Sabina worked for you until today," Tris pointed out incredulously. "What did she dissent from?"

"The guards who came to arrest her," Dolorin said. "She went against my orders by not returning to work, and then she tried to disobey the guards. That is dissent, and you know better than most that it needs to be stomped out immediately. You helped my father with the harenid uprising."

His eyebrow arched sharply. "Or do you no longer have the stomach for that, Tristitia?"

She lowered her gaze. "No, of course, I do, Sire. I only wish to serve my Master by advising your properly."

"Well, you have, and now you can keep quiet and do as I say," the King snapped.

"Yes, Sire," she said. "What do you wish for me to do?"

"Go oversee the guards," Dolorin commanded. "Ensure they're getting every single faun, and that they're searching everywhere for Luxuria and Castimonia."

She nodded once. "Yes, Sire."

Because she had nothing more to say, nothing more that she wanted to hear, she turned and marched out of the throne room before another word was uttered.

The guards didn't need her, and she turned and headed down the hallway toward her chancery. She hadn't made it very far when Ira ran and caught up with her.

"What are we going to do about Sabina?" he asked in a hushed voice.

"Nothing. She's in the dungeon," Tris replied flatly.

"But we can't just leave her there," Ira insisted. "She's our friend."

"She *was*. Now she's the enemy of the kingdom," she said. "Things change fast in Desperationis."

"You're going to stand by and let her be executed?"

She took a fortifying breath and kept her eyes straight ahead. "I will do what's needed of me. I always have."

"What happened with the uprising under the King's father?" Ira asked. "Dolorin has brought it up a few times."

"His father Dolian was smarter than Dolorin, but twice as impatient," Tris said.

Ira looked at her expectantly, and she plunged ahead, telling him the story of the greatest mistake of her life:

When he was a young King many years ago, before the fauns immigrated here, the ones who did the grunt work around the city were mostly the harenids.

Harenids were desert nymphs. They were petite, no more than three feet tall, and otherwise human in appearance. Both the men and women were sinewy and wore their hair long, and despite their small size, they were strong and resilient.

The harenids had lived in the harsh Morsenea Desert for centuries, but it had grown too unhospitable even for them, so they had moved into the city.

At first, it seemed to work well for everyone. The harenids worked, and in return, they were paid enough to have small homes and enough food.

But the famines of northern Cormundie affected the food supply everywhere, and greed has always been a powerful motivator for kings and queens anyway.

King Dolian decided to pay them less. He figured that since the harenids were so small, and relatively impoverished, they would be unable to fight back.

The harenids, though, were fiercely loyal. When one of them was mistreated, they were all mistreated. They went on strike, refusing to work until they were paid what they were owed.

Dolian sent the King's men after them, but the harenids were used to fighting leviathans. They knew how to handle themselves against the sonneillons. It was a brutal, bloody fight in the streets, and the harenids were winning.

Tris had advised Dolian to leave their pay as it was, but when he didn't listen, she advised him to strike back with a big show of force. She wanted it to be over quickly, but the harenids were not so easily defeated.

After the third day of blood in the streets, the head of the harenids approached, asking for a truce. If Dolian agreed to their previous pay, all of this could be forgotten, and they would return to work.

But the King could never forget the harenids had risen up against him. The fighting had already gone on too long, and he had realized his mistake, though he could never admit it.

The fighting would only stop if he agreed to the terms, and he could only agree to them if he got his pound of flesh as well. The harenids had to take a punishment, beyond the lives that had been lost.

So Tris proposed a compromise. Take one of the harenids – the leader of the uprising – and kill him in a spectacle for everyone to see. Leave his head on a spike, and no one would dare to go up against the King again.

Dolian loved the idea, and he called a meeting in the palace courtyard. Tris joined the King, along with all the sonneillon and human guards, and then all the harenids arrived. The King told them that they could choose their leader to sacrifice, and the leader would be executed the following day in front of the city.

The harenids thought about it for only a moment, and then, one by one, they all began raising their hands and declaring themselves "the leader." They refused to sacrifice even one of them.

Tris didn't know if they believed Dolian would back down and let them all live, or if they knew how things would transpire. But they all stood together, every man, woman, and child of the harenids.

So the King looked to Tristitia, and he asked, "What should I do?"

Because she wanted it over with, and because Tris didn't truly know what would happen, she told him, "Do as you see fit, Sire."

Dolian had smiled then, a cheeky grin, and he turned to face the crowd of volunteering harenids. He still smiled as he announced, "Kill them all."

The harenids had been good fighters, but they had not gone to the palace to fight. They were under armed, surrounded by sonneillons with spears and swords, and the exits were all blocked.

Tris tried to backtrack and advise the King against it, but it was too late. The command had been given. Once it began, there was nothing she could do, except watch as harenids were slaughtered.

A few sonneillons fell with them, but in the end, the harenids were extinct, and Dolian was still King.

He outsourced the labor, paying top dollar to pirates to recruit servants from their travels.

"I gave the King advice for a peaceful solution, and it was a bloodbath," she finished her story.

"So you're going to stand by and do nothing to help Sabina?" Ira asked. "Because you're afraid?"

"No, I'm going to be very careful so I never have that much blood on my hands ever again."

CHAPTER TWENTY-FIVE

THE DUNGEONS OF THE EMERALD PALACE were as dank and dark as any Indy had seen, though these were far more crowded than most. Each cell was hardly the width of a carriage. Three walls made of stone and the fourth made of bars to remind them they were all in a cage.

Most of them were fauns, but he could also see the odd human, woodsprite, witch, and even a pair of ogres. Dozens of them packed inside each cage.

The guards had brought Indy down to a smaller cell, not large enough for more than a few. Sabina, the blonde faun he'd met last night, was already there.

Her eyes were red-rimmed and desperate, and they widened when the sonneillons threw him in with her. She was sitting in the far corner of the cell, below the small slit of a window in the stone wall. When he stumbled in, she hurried over to help him.

Indy had put up quite a fight when he saw the Desperationis soldiers and sonneillons rounding up the folk of Little Faunton. He couldn't look away and let harm come to them, but he had been overpowered, as he'd known he would be when he saw so many King's men with sharp spiked pilums and double-edged swords. Twenty of them had descended upon Indy, and a lone virtu – even a powerful one like him – hadn't stood a chance.

In his many years as the Industria, fighting on the side of Good had sometimes come to actual physical blows. The beating the King's men had given him wasn't the worst he'd gotten, but he was bloodied, bruised, and horrified.

Sabina tore off a swatch of fabric from her dress, and she gently dabbed at the wounds on his face and forehead. "Did they do this because you helped us in Little Faunton?"

He grimaced. "No. The guards recognized me as a virtu."

She froze, her eyes darting to his. She hadn't known before what he was. "But Desperationis belongs to Valefor."

"He's not here, and the kingdom is in danger," Indy explained tiredly. "I came here to help, but the King is far more volatile than I thought."

"In Tris's absence, the King has been talking to Valefor and Mephis so much, and…" She lowered her hands and looked away. "Well, it hasn't been good."

Indy looked at the cell across from them. Young faun children, little more than babies, cried softly as they clung to each other.

"I don't understand how your King could do this. Caging his own people, and over something as trivial as repairing their homes after a disaster," he said.

"He's never considered us his people." Sabina leaned back against the wall across from him, her arms folded over her chest. "Because we came from Desiderium during the famine.

"We've never done anything wrong," she went on, and she exhaled roughly. "He's looking for an excuse, because of the sangcoranimilia."

Indy was aghast. "*The sangcoranimilia?*"

It was an ancient rite done to purify the land, but it required a sacrifice so great that it was almost never performed anymore. The ritual needed many, many mortal beings to be obliterated in a vicious ceremony, where they were made to surrender everything – blood, body, and soul. To do so necessitated powerful sorcery to part the blood and soul from the flesh, and all would be consumed in fire and magic.

"Your king isn't powerful enough to do that," Indy said, more because he hoped it to be true than that he actually believed it.

"I overheard the King talking to one of the sonneillon," Sabina said in a low voice, so the others wouldn't hear. "They've found a sorceress who will arrive soon. She'll perform the sangcoranimilia, and that will clear the land for Valefor's return."

Indy leaned back against the wall, the enormity of the situation crashing down on him. His eyes were on the filthy floor, but his mind was racing through all the possibilities to find any way he could prevent it.

"Rounding you all up like this wasn't just show of force," he said in a low voice. "He means to kill you. But a mad King won't stop there."

Everyone in Desperationis was in danger as long as Dolorin was in power. The fauns were the easiest target because they hadn't been here that long. But the soldiers had called Reni a "water faun" before she escaped, and they would come after her soon enough.

The King's men were already looking for Lux and Lily because of that damned carriage, and they had seen Indy with Reni, so it was only a matter of time before they found them with Tris.

The King would arrest them all, and almost certainly, he would kill them. Even Tristitia. Valefor could replace her with someone more loyal.

"We can't stay here," Indy said. "We must escape."

"I agree, but I can't see how." Sabina motioned to the stone and bars that surrounded them.

Through the narrow window – no more than two inches tall and maybe a foot wide – the wind began to howl. Indy looked over at the storm brewing outside, and an idea occurred to him.

He went back toward the bars and outstretched his arms between them. The floor of the dungeons appeared to be a muddy mixture of dirt and filth stamped smooth by so many feet walking on it.

As he moved his hands subtly in the air, he summoned the power he had within him. Gradually, the air began to shift around them, as a breeze picked up.

Indy conjured the wind, so it became a small swirling cyclone. It picked up lighter bits of debris – dust, straw, a pebble or two – but it wasn't powerful enough to do more.

Gritting his teeth, he focused all his energy toward it. The cyclone spun faster, causing enough wind that it ruffled the hair of the fauns watching him.

In order for them to escape, he needed the wind strong enough to loosen the ground beneath the cells. He wanted to use his power to excavate a way out beneath the walls.

But there wasn't enough space for the cyclone to grow without hurting anyone, and he was exhausted from the beating he'd already taken today.

Try as he might to contain the wind and make an escape, he was losing it. The muscles in his arms and hands were constricting, his fingers clenched into claws, and his head was throbbing. His heart felt as if it were going to explode, but he refused to quit.

Until his body gave out. All at once, the windstorm dissipated, and he collapsed to the ground on his knees. When he rested his forehead against the bars, sweat ran into his eyes, and he felt blood dripping from his nose.

"Don't kill yourself to save us," Sabina said, and she put a comforting hand on his trembling shoulder.

"I can't find a way out," he said breathlessly.

"Then we'll find another way," she assured him. "We won't die today."

CHAPTER TWENTY-SIX

TRIS MOVED QUIETLY THROUGH THE PALACE and stuck to the shadows, though she didn't necessarily need to. The usual guards were busy patrolling the city outside the palace for fauns and dissenters.

Her only real obstacle getting down to the dungeon had been losing Ira. He had seemed intent on sticking with her, arguing with her about everything, but she couldn't tell him what she planned to do. Not when his loyalties still seemed so close to Valefor.

In her long tenure as a consiliarius, she had often surreptitiously disobeyed a King or gone behind his back. But she had never done anything so overtly treasonous before today.

She sent away the sonneillons guarding the entrance of the dungeon, telling them that they were needed in the city to help with the arrests. They were eager to see the action and didn't even question why she was the one giving such a command.

The keys were left on a ring hanging by the door, and Tris grabbed them before marching through the rows and rows of weeping fauns. She didn't pause or look at them. There wasn't much time, and she couldn't waste any of it on pity.

She felt him before she saw him. A pull towards the final cell, where she knew she'd find him waiting.

"*Tris*." Indy breathed her name in relief, and his hands gripped the bars tightly. His face was covered in drying and darkening bruises, and his hands were scabbed and swollen.

She put her hand over his, because she needed to touch him, to feel his cool skin against hers, to know that he was alive in a tangible way.

"What have they done to you?" she asked.

"It doesn't matter," he said brusquely. "You have to get the fauns out of here. The King's going to kill everyone."

"No, I will talk him out of that." She shook her head and let go of him. "I won't let that happen."

"Valefor needs them for the sangcoranimilia," he whispered.

Tris was already unlocking his cell, but she flinched when she heard the word. It was a taboo ritual, rarely done because of the sheer brutality of the sacrifice.

"Dolorin's not ready for something like that," she said, but it was a weak argument. She knew that he had the stomach for such a thing, but he wasn't powerful enough. He would need a master of sorcery, and he didn't have any in his court.

With the cell finally unlocked, she opened the door. She wanted to pull Indy into her arms and kiss him, ignoring all the onlookers, and just for a moment relish that he was safe and alive and hers.

But when she went to embrace him, he reached for the keys. He took them from her before she had any time to protest.

"Start freeing the rest of them," he commanded as he handed the keys to Sabina. Tris hadn't even noticed her there, not until then.

"No, I hadn't meant to let them all go," Tris said. "The King will release them. I will see to it, but –"

"I'm not letting them sit in cages while you attempt to argue civility to a mad King." Indy put a hand on her arm, firm but kind, holding her in place as Sabina slipped by.

"I don't want them to die either, but what life will they have when they step foot outside this palace?" Tris argued in a hushed voice so the prisoners would not be able to hear. "They can't go back to Little Faunton. They'll have to sneak out of the city without the King's men finding them, with little to no money or possessions."

"But they will be alive!" Indy shot back. "They will die if they stay. Valefor and your King are growing desperate. This needs to be done."

"He's not my King, and I won't stop you," Tris said vehemently. "But this will not end without bloodshed."

"It is worth the risk," Indy persisted.

She looked into his eyes, dark and gray as an angry storm cloud. "I know."

"Tristitia, what are you doing?" Ira asked, and she looked over to see him standing in the entrance of the dungeon, watching as Sabina opened the cages.

"The King arrested me," Sabina said. She was speaking to Ira, but she never slowed or stopped her work of unlocking the cells. "He's going to kill us all, Ira. We have to escape."

"You can go and pretend you didn't see any of this," Tris told him. "I won't tell the King you were here."

Ira stepped to the side, letting the fauns that had been freed scurry past him. He walked over to Sabina and helped her open a cell door.

Tris turned back to Indy, speaking low so the others wouldn't overhear. "When you get out of here, go find Reni. She'll be able to get some of them on a ship, I'm sure. I'll go to the King and keep him busy, and then I'll tell him that I got word the fauns were making their escape across the desert. He'll waste time searching in the opposite direction."

"Why don't you come with us?" Indy asked.

"No. If you're freeing all the prisoners, I have to misdirect the King if they are to have any chance of getting away."

He put his hand on her cheek. "I will come back for you once they're safe."

"Don't," she said thickly, and it hurt to say it. "If Dolorin means to do a sangcoranimilia, then Desperationis will be very unsafe for the likes of you. I have to stay to talk him out of it, and... and you should return to the Castimonia. Isn't that as your Mistress wants?"

His eyes bounced down to her lips, then to her eyes again. "We will find each other again."

"I know." She smiled sadly at him. "Now go, help them escape. Ira and Sabina will need you."

Tris turned and walked away, because if she didn't, she might ask him to stay. She took a deep breath and steeled her spine as she headed up to the throne room.

CHAPTER TWENTY-SEVEN

AS LILY WATCHED OUT THE WINDOW at the dark clouds and angry seas, she thought back to the nightmare she'd had.

So far, she'd told no one of it, not even Maxon. When she awoke in the middle of the night, trembling and covered in a cold sweat, she had leapt out of bed and dried herself before disturbing him.

He asked her what was wrong, of course, but she had lied to him, because she hadn't wanted to worry him. Not on their honeymoon. They were in a rented chateau in Insontia, and she told Maxon that they couldn't indulge in their wealth when others were suffering.

That was how they'd ended up on the house on the Vespertine Sea, with storms brewing on every front.

While she did worry about the Desperationians, her true impetus had been the terrible dream that had felt more like a vision.

She was in Luminelle's home, but the usual pristine white marble was broken and destroyed. The flowers were withered, the grass was on fire, the fountains were dry. The air smelled of brimstone and lilacs, and feathers and ashes rained down from the sky.

As Lily slowly walked through the ruins, she could hear people weeping, but she couldn't see them.

It was a far-off echo, and over that, she heard the sound of an infant crying.

She ran through the palace, jumping over collapsed marble pillars, desperate to find the wailing baby.

Finally, Lily reached the conservatory. The glass ceilings were broken, and shattered glass was littered all over the dead and dying plants. In the very center of the room, lying on a bed of dried flower petals, was the tiny baby.

She was such a precious thing, even with her face scrunched up and red as she screamed. The baby was lying on her back, but Lily could see two delicate wings made of light coming out from behind her.

Lily crouched down before the little girl and touched her tiny foot. "What are you doing here, sweet girl?"

Suddenly, a voice boomed all around, rattling the walls like thunder, and the sky above turned black. "*You will have to choose – her, or the world?*"

"Luminelle?" Lily called for her Mistress, but no one responded. The walls were still shaking, the earth beneath her feet felt like it was about to give. "Luminelle, what is happening? What shall I do?"

The only reply came in the angry booming voice again: "*No one can save you.*"

That's when Lily had awoken in the cold sweat. Even as so much time passed since then, she couldn't shake off the dream.

"Lily?" Maxon asked, and by the concern in his voice, she realized he must've been saying her name multiple times.

She smiled wanly up at him. "Did you need something?"

168

"Are you doing okay?" He glanced over to where Reni was anxiously pacing nearby and lowered his voice. "Really. How are you?"

"I am scared, and I am upset about the mess of things," she replied honestly. "But I am otherwise fine. There's no need to fret over me."

Reni had been in a state since she'd returned, not that Lily blamed her. What she'd been through with the King's men assaulting her sounded horrible, and both she and Maxon had been trying to calm the distressed weremer.

Maxon had returned to patching up the roof, but with the storm moving in so soon, he didn't have time to nail the boards. He'd closed it up with blankets and tarps, so at least the house had some protection from the elements.

Until a few minutes ago, Lily had been helping by talking to Reni. She had made a pot of tea and asked her about her life at the sea, and while Reni only gave short answers and barely sipped the tea, she did calm some.

But then Lily had gotten distracted by the weather out the window, and the darkening of the clouds had reminded her of her nightmare again. When the thunder rumbled, she could almost swear she heard the words, "*No one can save you.*"

Now she was back in the present, and Reni had returned to making agitated circles around the house, so Lily had work to do.

"Reni, you must have seen so many amazing things in the sea," Lily said. "How far have you gone?"

"The Eurous Sea," Reni replied absently. "What do you think is taking Tris so long? Why hasn't she come back?"

"It can't be quick getting prisoners released," Lily said, which sounded reasonable enough, but it didn't make her any less worried, either.

"What weapons do you have, Reni?" Maxon asked suddenly, and his eyes were fixed on the window facing the mainland.

"What kind of question is that?" Lily asked.

"The kind I ask when sonneillons are marching up the bridge toward the house right now," Maxon said.

CHAPTER TWENTY-EIGHT

KING DOLORIN WAS IN HIS THRONE ROOM, as he so
often was, but he wasn't sitting in his chair. The
southern wall was open to the city and sea, and he
stood in front of it, watching as the dark clouds settled
over his kingdom.

Tris came into the room, her boots echoing softly
on the stone, but he didn't turn. His back was to her,
with his arms folded behind him, and his gaze was on
the city.

"Some of the sonneillons fear that this storm will
bring another procello," the King said as she
approached him. "But I know differently."

"How do you know such things?" she asked as
she joined him.

"Our Master has told me," Dolorin replied with a
confident smile. "We will do as he says, and we will
be spared. He's told me of a ritual so that he can
return and protect us."

"A *ritual*," Tris repeated and grimaced. "So it's
true then? You're planning on the sangcoranimilia?"

He tilted his head, looking surprised but pleased.
"How have you already heard of it?"

"The sonneillons can be quite the gossips."

"That is unfortunately true," he agreed with a
sigh. "But my point remains. We will be safe. No one
in Desperationis has to worry."

"Except the fauns, you mean," Tris corrected
him.

The King swatted away her words as if they were flies. "The fauns have never truly been a part of Desperationis anyway. They've been a drain on our kingdom for long enough. It's time they give back."

She set her jaw and tried to think of the words to sway him. So many times, she had managed to convince him and his father to avoid bloodshed by the skin of her teeth. But this time....

Dolorin had never looked so certain, or so delighted about it. He was practically giddy telling her of his plans and his conversations with Valefor.

What if she could not change his mind? What would she do if he was intent on massacring innocents to bring back Valefor?

"Sire!" Mephis's shrill voice echoed from the corridor, and Tris cringed inwardly. His hooves clacked on the stone floors as he ran. "Sire!"

"Yes, yes, what is it?" the King asked when the sonneillon hurried breathlessly into the room.

"The fauns..." Mephis said between gasps for air. "They're all gone."

"*Gone*?" King Dolorin questioned. "You mean we've gotten them all?"

"No, Sire, the dungeon is *empty*," Mephis said.

Tris hoped they'd have more time before anyone realized the fauns were gone. They wouldn't have made it to Reni, not quite yet, but they would be close. If they moved quick enough.

"*What*?" Dolorin snapped. "How could that be?"

"All the cells were open, as if someone just... set them free," Mephis explained in disbelief.

The King had been staring down at the simpering minion, but now he slowly turned his head to look at Tris. She tried to keep her face neutral, to not let anything show, but she could see the wheels turning as he studied her.

"You didn't want me to kill the fauns, did you?" Dolorin asked her.

"I thought it was drastic and would cause more problems for you down the line," Tris admitted evenly. "I am only thinking about the fate of the kingdom and your dynasty."

"But Valefor – *our Master* – has told me to kill them all." He stepped closer to her, his dark eyes suspicious and his words taunting. "Why would you stand in the way of that? Why would you disobey your Master?"

"I'm not," she argued. "I am merely trying to advise –"

His expression suddenly fell, and he shook his head in disappointment. "My father always spoke so highly of you, Tristitia. It's a true shame, because you have been nothing but a failure to me."

"I have advised you as well as –"

"You are not loyal to me, you are not loyal to Valefor, and frankly, I am tired of your guidance," he cut her off sharply.

Tris took a step back and licked her lips. "I am sorry that you feel that –"

Suddenly, he reached over and grabbed the irin-bone dagger Mephis always wore on his belt. Before Tris could even register what he'd done, the King grabbed her. He put his arm around her – his hand on the small of her back, as if they were lovers – and he pulled her close. She put her hands on his chest to push him away, and then she felt the blade.

It was cold and sharp sliding between her ribs, and heat blossomed inside her chest. There was pain. An abstract burning that consumed the dark recesses

173

of her mind, but mostly, what she felt was her life slipping out from her, like sand between her fingers.

"I am sorry, Tris, but it is past time for us to find a replacement," Dolorin said.

He pulled the knife from her, and she gasped. He lowered her to the floor, and then she was lying alone on cold stone. Her mouth opened and closed, but she couldn't find words. Tears formed in her eyes, blurring the ceiling above her, and Tris realized that would be the last thing she saw before she died.

CHAPTER TWENTY-NINE

"I HAD A BIG CHEST OF WEAPONS," Reni muttered as she handed Maxon a stick with rusty nails protruding out of it. "But it was against the wall that went out to the sea, so I don't have any handy."

"We can make do with these," Maxon said, as if he had ever been good in a fight, even when he had a proper weapon.

Three sonneillons were marching up the bridge right to the front door, likely on their way to haul Reni to the dungeons, and they would be thrilled to get their hands on another virtu and the traitorous peccati.

Back in his time as the Luxuria, Maxon had dealt with the sonneillons too often. Despite the fact that they looked like decaying daemons, they were surprisingly strong and fast when they needed to be.

He glanced over at Lily, standing beside him and wielding a cleaver. Her jaw was set, and her eyes were determined. Even in her dress, with ribbons in her dark hair, she was fierce.

But the sonneillon were likely stronger.

"Go in one of the back rooms to hide, so you'll be safe," he told her. "Let me and Reni face them head on."

She shook her head. "I am fighting by your side. I will not let you face any monsters alone."

175

"I have an idea," Reni declared when the enemy was nearly at the door. She was backing away, toward the wall that was repaired with broken boards and tarps. "If you need me, try to get them into the water."

"Okay?" Maxon said uncertainly, because there wasn't time for anything more.

Reni slipped out between the boards and tarps just as the sonneillons started pounding down the front door.

Maxon was holding his weaponized stick like a sword, while Lily stood a bit further into the house, holding the cleaver in one hand and a cast iron pot in the other.

The door flew open, and the first sonneillon entered and announced, "We're here on orders from the King –" But Maxon didn't let him say anymore.

He swung the stick right at his head, and one of the rusted nails drove straight into the yellowed eyeball of the sonneillon. There was a sickening wet sound as the weapon collided with the creature, but it was quickly drowned out by the shrieks of the sonneillon.

Another sonneillon charged in right behind the first, and he immediately went after Maxon. He jumped onto his back, wrapping his long arms around Maxon's throat.

"Get off him!" Lily screamed, and she raised her hands up.

Wind filled the room – blowing her hair and dress, ruffling the tarps securing the holes – and then she directed it all at the sonneillon.

He flew backwards, slamming hard into the wall. Maxon coughed and rubbed his throat, and when the sonneillon tried to stand, Lily knocked it back again with her wind.

Maxon pulled his stick with nails out of the dead sonneillon, and then he walked over to the one that Lily had trapped against the wall. It only took two good hits, and the sonneillon was dead.

The final sonneillon stood in the doorway, yelling at them to comply. The wind had calmed down, and Lily looked pale and breathless from the exertion of conjuring it. She couldn't summon the wind again, not so soon.

She rushed straight at the sonneillon and pushed it out the front door. The sonneillon tripped and fell backwards onto the wet rock the house was built on, and she fell down with him.

"Lily!" Maxon shouted, and he was instantly at her side. He took her arm, helping her to her feet, but the sonneillon reached out and caught onto her dress. He lay at the edge of the rock, slipping to the sea.

From the water just beyond the brink, Reni suddenly burst up. She wrapped her arms around the sonneillon's neck, and he let out an anguished cry as she grabbed him.

The sonneillon refused to let go of Lily's dress, and the fabric tore as Reni pulled him under. Maxon held fast onto Lily, afraid that the weremer would accidentally pull her down with the enemy.

Once he was sure that she was safe, Maxon leaned forward and peered down at the sea. The water churned and crashed against the rock, and he couldn't see anything.

"Should we jump in to help her?" Lily asked.

"I think if we went in, we'd drown," Maxon reasoned. "The mermaid can handle it."

So they stood hand-in-hand, waiting for her to surface, as the winds raged around them. The clouds were dark and swirling, and soon the rain would come.

Just when Maxon was about to suggest they go inside to wait for Reni, she appeared. Her head popped out of the water, and she was holding a large pirate sword between her teeth.

She gripped onto the rock and stretched her hands up toward them. Maxon took one, and Lily took the other, and they both pulled her up out of the water, mindful of the sword.

The top half of Reni's body was as it had been before she went into the sea, but from her waist down was a fish tail covered in iridescent green scales. On closer look, Maxon realized that a few scales were dotted on her arms, chest, and neck.

Once she was sitting on the rock, Reni took the blade from her mouth. "I went looking for my weapons that had gone under, and I only managed to find this one. But I killed the sonneillon." She glanced between Maxon and Lily. "You handled the other two okay?"

"Yes, we took care of them," Lily said. "I've faced off against sonneillons before. They're terrifying to look at, but they're not that hard to dispatch."

"You've got yourself quite the force of nature," Reni remarked to Maxon.

He smiled at his wife. "I know. I'm a lucky man."

Reni's tail slowly shifted, splitting into two legs covered in tawny skin. The baggy blouse she'd been wearing easily hid her more private parts, but she went inside and put on dry clothes.

The house was in a disarray from the fighting, and Lily immediately set about cleaning it up. Upon

Reni's suggestion, Maxon lugged the corpses outside and kicked them into the sea.

"Something will eat them down there, and they won't go to waste," Reni told him.

She came out of her room freshly changed into a dry top and pants, and she ran her hand through her tangles of dark hair and braids.

"Do you think Tris will return soon?" Lily asked.

Reni sat down in a chair that Lily had just righted. "I don't know. But you're not safe here anymore. The sonneillon came for me or you, it doesn't really matter. Eventually, more will come when they realize that the others have not returned, and they will keep coming, until they capture you or we've killed them all."

"How many sonneillons are here in Desperationis?" Lily asked.

"More than even you can take on, Princess," Reni said with a smirk.

"Tris told us that our horses were stabled nearby," Maxon said. "Could we take them and go?"

"We can't leave without knowing that Indy is safe," Lily protested.

"And what if he isn't?" Maxon asked gently. "What do you propose the two of us do against the King and all his men?"

Lily frowned and asked, "What would you do if it were me? If I were the one in the dungeon instead of Indy?"

"I would do everything and anything to get you back, even if it was a suicide mission," Maxon admitted. "So those are not the choices that I think we should make here."

"Reni, what do you think we should do?" Lily asked.

Reni had been sitting on her chair, cleaning the sword she had rescued from the sea, and she looked up at Lily's question. Her mouth opened, like she meant to answer, but then her eyes widened and she got to her feet.

"What?" Lily asked.

"Open the door," Reni replied cryptically.

Maxon turned to follow Reni's gaze out the window, but Lily was already rushing over to do as Reni said.

On the long bridge from the mainland, a line of fauns were walking. They were battered and dirty, many of them limping and bleeding.

In Desiderium where he had grown up, Maxon had known plenty of fauns. Most of them were hardworking and peaceful, and seeing the realities of their unjust imprisonment was alarming.

"*Indy!*" Lily squealed with delight.

She hugged Indy in the doorway. He didn't look any better than the fauns, and Maxon felt a flash of guilt.

He had only been thinking of Lily, of keeping her safe and getting her out of the dangerous situation in Desperationis. But as he watched her and Indy embracing, Maxon realized how selfish he was being.

"I am very happy to see you've escaped, but what are you all doing here?" Reni asked. "This isn't a safe house. The sonneillons were just here."

A blond faun had been standing beside Indy, and she stepped into the house and extended her hand toward Reni. "I'm Sabina, and I was the seneschal. We need to get passage out of here before the King slaughters us all."

Reni waited a beat, then nodded. "Okay. I know of some ships."

Reni and Sabina went into the logistics of getting so many fauns on a ship during a storm in short order. All without any real funds.

Lily immediately offered up her jewelry, anything she had on her that was worth anything – a sapphire necklace, a diamond bracelet, a many-jeweled butterfly broach, everything but her wedding ring.

All the while, Indy had been standing by, listening and interjecting if he had anything to add. Until he abruptly doubled over, and his face had blanched underneath the bruises.

"Indy, are you okay?" Lily put her hand on his back and crouched beside him. "What's wrong?"

Indy grimaced and groaned, but didn't answer right away. When he finally did, it was just a low whisper, *"Tris."*

"Where is Tris?" Reni asked.

Indy straightened up. "I have to get her. She... she needs me."

"What? How do you know that?" Lily asked.

"Where is she?" Reni repeated.

The pain seemed to be subsiding, because Indy was looking closer to normal, with the color returning to his cheeks.

"Stay here and take care of the fauns. I'll go and get Tris," Indy told Reni, then he looked to Lily. "I won't come back without her. So... if I don't come back, don't wait for me. You and Maxon need to get out of here."

"What do you mean *if* you don't come back?" Lily asked.

He put his hand on her shoulder. "You are a good Castimonia. Keep up with training, and go back to Insontia. It's been an honor being your mentor."

181

"You can't just leave like this," Lily protested.

Indy smiled down at her, then he kissed her forehead. With that, he headed out the door, running toward the mainland and to Tris.

CHAPTER THIRTY

AS SOON AS HE'D FELT THE PAIN in his chest, sharp and hot, he'd known it was *her*. When Indy doubled over, it had been her name on his tongue.

Tris. He wanted to repeat it over and over as he ran, as if it were an incantation that could protect her. The world moved past him in a blur of images. Glimpses of a city in chaos. Sonneillons fighting the townsfolk. Buildings on fire. The King had tried for a massacre but ended up with a civil war.

Indy didn't have to think about where he was going. His body just knew.

There was a tether between him and Tris. He had felt it the moment he'd met her, but he had been trying to deny it. He could no longer pretend that the way he was drawn to her, the magnetic pull he felt toward her, no matter how near or far she might be, was part of any normal attraction.

This was unlike anything he'd ever felt in his life. When they had made love, her heart beat inside of his own, as if they were one.

He could feel her heart now, pounding slow and weak. It was as if she was fading, and that was an especially acute agony. Like his viscera was being ripped slowly out, and an angry fire consumed him.

Thunder rumbled overhead, and the rain that had been threatening finally descended. It fell in cold sheets, and Indy barely even noticed.

The chaos of the streets left the palace under-guarded. There were a few sonneillons by the main door, but the tether pulled Indy to a side entrance, hidden behind vines and moss.

He ran through the palace. It was a maze of stone corridors, dimly lit with torches, but his feet carried him straight to the throne room.

"There must be something useful we can make with a peccati body," King Dolorin was saying. "We need to preserve her so when the sorceress gets here, she can make use of it."

Indy entered the room, and the rest of the world fell away. All he could see was *her*, lying alone on the floor in a pool of her own blood.

Then he saw the King in his twisted crown, standing over her, with his sonneillon advisor Mephis beside him. They pondered Tris as if she were a piece of meat, and his vision darkened.

"Get away from her," Indy growled, and Dolorin and Mephis looked up at him in surprise.

"How did you get up here?" the King asked, and he sounded confused but unafraid.

"*Get away from her!*" Indy shouted.

This time, the King flinched, and Mephis actually took a step back from Tris.

"Who are you?" the King asked.

"He's the Industria!" Mephis hissed.

"Why are you bothered?" the King asked, completely baffled. "She is your lifelong enemy. Have I not done you a favor?"

The throne room was surprisingly bare, aside from a few tapestries on the wall, and a giant throne made of strong leviathan bones. Around the tall back, the bones were fanned out with sharpened points.

Indy started toward it and the King immediately began calling after him.

"Where are you going? Stay away from there. That throne isn't for you."

Indy grabbed one of the sharpest looking bones and started pulling.

"Stop that!" King Dolorin shouted, then quieter, "Mephis, stop him! My father made that throne!"

Indy ignored them, but when Mephis started charging toward him, he held out his hand. A burst of wind shot out and slammed into Mephis.

The sonneillon shrieked and his hooves screeched as they dragged on the floor, but he never slowed. The wind was strong enough that it took him through the curtains, out onto the balcony, and right over the edge.

"What do you think you're doing?" the King yelled. "I am the King of Desperationis, and my Master is Valefor."

"I do not give a damn about your Master," Indy said.

With one final pull, he got the sharpened bone free from the throne, and he turned to face the King.

"Well... you must care about something," the King faltered, when he realized that intimidation would not work.

"I cared about one thing very much," Indy admitted as he stalked toward the King. "But you killed her." "

King Dolorin shook his head in disbelief, as if he couldn't imagine that anyone would care about Tris. "You care for her? *Why?*"

"Because she's magnificent, and she is better than you in every single way."

The King started to blubber or blabber, it didn't matter anymore. While the King cowered before him, begging for his life and offering him untold riches, Indy drove the bone straight through his neck, killing Dolorin instantly.

Finally, Indy collapsed beside Tris. Her eyes were blank, staring up ahead, and he couldn't feel her heartbeat.

He cradled her in his arms, holding her as close to him as he could, and the heat was already fading from her body. He pressed his cheek against hers, and he wailed.

A guttural sound like a dying beast came from inside him, echoing through the empty room.

"No, I can't lose you," he said in a husky voice when his throat had gone raw from screaming. "I can't, I can't, *I won't.*"

He wept as he closed her eyelids and brushed the hair back from his face. "I love you, Tristitia. I love you with love beyond love. From the moment I met you, I was yours.

"And I can't... I cannot lose you now, not when we've only just found each other. We were meant to be together, Tris, and I can't..."

He looked up at the ceiling, shouting to the sky and beyond, to the other realms. "Luminelle, you can't let it end this way! Please, this is a mistake! You must return her!"

From the corner of the room, Indy heard a strange bubbling sound, and he saw the obsidian cauldron glowing green.

"Luminelle isn't listening," said a satiny voice from the cauldron. "But *I* am."

Indy had never spoken to him before, but he knew it was Valefor.

"Can you return her?" Indy asked.

"For a price."

He looked down at Tris, lifeless in his arms. A suffocating torment enveloped him, and he could not go on if she didn't live. It was more than the misery; it was an impossibility. He could not survive without her any more than he could survive without his own heart.

Indy bent down and gently kissed her forehead. His tears dampened her skin, and as he brushed them away, he said, "My heart is your heart, my life is your life, my soul will share your fate."

Still looking down at her, he said in a loud clear voice, "If you return her to me, I will vow my heart and soul to you, Valefor. I will promise to serve you for the rest of my life."

"You have already taken your vows, so that is little more than words to me," the cauldron bubbled in response. "But I am watching you, and I can see all that you do. I will save Tristitia for you now, and I will gladly take her from you again if you displease me."

Indy exhaled roughly. "I am yours, Valefor, now and forever, if you return her to me."

"So be it."

The cauldron fell silent. The room was still and quiet, aside from the rain outside. And Tris was motionless in his arms.

Then he felt it – a subtle heartbeat inside his own. His breath caught in his throat, and her eyes fluttered open.

Tris was alive.

CHAPTER THIRTY-ONE

THE FIRST THING SHE SAW were his eyes, gray and broken. Tears streamed down his cheeks, but he smiled down at her.

"*Indy?*" Tris asked. Her voice was dry and brittle, and she coughed after choking the word out.

He helped her sit up, keeping one arm around her waist. "You're okay. You're going to be okay."

"What happened?" she asked after her coughing passed. She took in the room, with the King's body bleeding out a few feet from her.

"When I arrived, Dolorin had stabbed you," Indy explained. "So I killed him. Mephis tried to stop me, so I killed him, too."

She wanted to ask more, but there was a pain in her chest she couldn't quite explain. She touched her side, on her ribs, and her shirt was torn and stained with blood, but there was no wound.

"What happened to my injuries?" she asked and looked up at him.

"I healed you by channeling my virtu energy," he said in a flat voice.

"I didn't know you could do that."

He put his hand on her face, caressing her cheek gently with his thumb. "I would do anything for you. I would burn this kingdom to the ground just to keep you warm." His throat bobbed as he swallowed, and his words came out thick. "I can't lose you, Tris. I love you."

"I love you, too, and I'm not going anywhere."

His mouth found hers then, and his lips were tentative and gentle. She clung to him and kissed him fiercely.

When they parted, he exhaled, and she breathed him in.

"We should go, though, before someone realizes you've killed the King," she said.

"Who will be the ruler now?" Indy asked as he helped her to her feet.

"Dolorin had no heirs. The laws of the kingdom say the sonneillons and nobility will have a council and make a decision," Tris said. "If they don't blame me for his death, I will get to sit on it and help them choose."

"You will stay on in Desperationis?"

"I will, if I can. They need me. Did the fauns escape?"

"Reni was finding them ships when I left."

"Good," she said, relieved. "Hopefully, they will be safe wherever they are, and I can help pick a King who is less of a cruel monster."

"Hopefully," Indy repeated quietly.

"But first, we need to get out of the palace."

CHAPTER THIRTY-TWO

THE ESCAPE FROM THE EMERALD PALACE hadn't been as hard as Tris had feared because everyone was preoccupied with the storm. The recent procello left the kingdom on edge, even if this one wasn't as bad.

According to Indy, there had been fighting in the street, but it stopped as soon as the rain began. Everyone had ran for cover, sonneillons and townsfolk alike.

Tris and Indy made it back to an empty house. There were signs that others had been there, like muddy hoof prints left on the floor, but nobody was home.

A short note was tacked to the wall, written in lovely curly writing.

"Dear Indy and Tris,

Thank you both for all your help and hospitality. I hope to repay you both again soon. I wanted to stay until you returned, but I realized doing so would be dangerous for you. Reni will be back later and tell you how her side of things went, but Maxon and I have returned home. We're taking Velox and Addonexus, and we've left the carriage. Perhaps you can sell it or donate it.

Please write soon to let us know that you are well. In my heart, I am certain that you are, but I fear that's because I can't bear to think otherwise.

Take care until we can see each other again.

Sincerely yours,

191

Lily"

Tris read the note and handed it to Indy, then limped over to the hammock. She collapsed back into it, and Indy finished reading before joining her. They sat together, holding hands, and slowly rocking as the wind raged and rain dripped in around the tarps blocking the holes.

"Are you staying here?" she asked.

"Yes."

"Good." She curled up beside him and rested her head on his chest. His heartbeat was so much faster than hers.

He wrapped an arm around her and kissed the top of her head. "What happens next?"

"Well, next as in right now, we rest. That's as far as I know."

"Sounds perfect to me," Indy said, and they retired to her lumpy bed. When she offered to help put him to sleep, he didn't even protest.

They both slept and slept, long after Reni had come back and the storm had moved on. They slept entwined together, and when they awoke, they ate and they bathed, and they held hands and they tended to their wounds.

Reni told them about what she'd done, how she had gotten the fauns onto two different ships, paid for by the jewelry that Lily had provided.

After two days of rest, Tris got word that the sonneillons were convening to decide a new King, and she had a seat on the council. They believed that the fauns had assassinated him and Mephis, and now the fauns were long gone. Life was returning to normal, or at least as close to normal as anything had been since the Altering.

The night before the meeting of the sonneillons, Tris and Indy were relaxing in the hammock again. Reni had gone on a job out to sea, so they had the house to themselves.

"How long will you be able to stay with me?" Tris asked.

"As long as you'll let me," he replied.

"Aren't you needed in Insontia? Or doesn't Luminelle have other places for you to be?"

His expression darkened, and he looked away from her. The last couple days, he was silent and still, and she'd often catch him watching her with a strange smile on his face.

"I am where I am meant to be, and Luminelle knows that," he said evasively.

"What does that mean? Have you spoken to her?"

"No, but I will soon. There will be time to worry later," he murmured and brushed the hair back from her face. He kissed her gently and traced his fingers along her jaw. "Tomorrow there will be much to do, but tonight... tonight's just the two of us."

"I never would have thought you would be the one to suggest living in the moment," she teased. "But if the moment is with you, then I will not be one to argue."

She was smiling when her lips found his, and his arms wrapped around her. She pushed him back and climbed on top of him, straddling him between her legs –

– a knock at the front door interrupted them.

"Are you expecting anyone?" Indy asked.

"Not that I know of." She sighed as she stood up. "But I should answer it. It might be about tomorrow."

Indy moved more quickly than she did, so by the time she had trudged over to the door, he was

193

standing behind her with Reni's pirate sword in his hand.

CHAPTER THIRTY-THREE

AVARITIA WAS ON TRIS'S DOORSTEP. His hands were on his hips, and his head was tilted back as he appraised her home.

"I heard that you all got hit badly with a procello," he said. "But your place looks all right."

"Did you travel all the way here to inspect my house?" she asked dryly.

"Not at all." Ava finally looked at her, and then his dark eyes fell on Indy behind her, and his smile deepened. "Why don't you invite me in, and we can talk about it all?"

She stepped back. "You can come in, but I'm not calling it an invitation."

"You have always been one for semantics, Tris, but since it's your home, I shan't complain," he said as he came inside and shut the door behind him. "Industria, it's good to see you again."

"What are you doing here?" Indy asked, and his voice was hard and flat.

Tris wasn't exactly thrilled about Ava dropping in unannounced, but Indy seemed far more bothered than her. He glared at Ava, and his nostrils flared slightly as he inhaled.

"Should I ask you the same thing?" Ava countered with a knowing smirk. "Or have I already surmised what is transpiring between the two of you?"

195

"Ava, honestly, I'm tired and not up for playing games. Reni's out to sea, so there's no hope of her food," Tris said, and Ava frowned, genuinely disappointed about her roommate's absence. "What are you doing here?"

"Mind if I have a seat?" Ava was already pulling out a chair at the dining table, but he did pause and look to Tris for permission.

"Go right ahead," she said with a shrug.

He gave her a quick smile and sat back in the chair. Indy stood right behind her, slightly to the side, and she practically felt him glaring over her shoulder.

"Your King here was one of Valefor's closest allies on Cormundie," Ava said, as if she didn't already know that. "The Queen in Auctoritas seems to have lost interest since Valefor has been gone, and Furorem doesn't even have a King right now, since several different Lords are battling for the title. Many of the kingdoms are experiencing great upheaval, actually."

"The rumblings I've heard make that sound true enough, but then what makes Desperationis's upheaval so interesting to you?" Tris asked.

Indy pulled out a chair and sat down. The others had been lost in the procello, and Tris didn't want to be the only one standing, so she sat on Indy's lap.

Their relationship was evident to Ava, which meant there was no point in being coy. Indy looped a protective arm around her waist, holding her close to him, and though she felt no fear of Ava, there was something nice about knowing that Indy wouldn't let anything happen to her.

"Desperationis is set to appoint a new ruler, and you are on the council to decide who that will be," Ava said.

"How do you know that?" Tris asked in dismay, and Indy's arm around her tensed.

"I have friends, I like to talk, rumors have their way of finding me," Ava said with a dismissive wave of his fingers. "What matters is that I know that Valefor is counting on the kingdom of Desperationis to complete the sangcoranimilia ritual he needs to return." He leaned forward slightly and licked his bottom lip. "That's not something that would be good for you either, and I think you know that."

"Are you asking if I know the ritual that horrifically obliterates hundreds of beings out of existence is a bad thing?" she asked skeptically.

Ava shrugged. "With our kind, one can never be too sure where their moral compass points."

"Even Ira knows the sangcoranimilia is an abomination," Tris contended.

"That is wonderful," he replied with faux cheer. "Do you know where Ira is?"

She stiffened. The last time she had seen Ira, the King had still been alive. Ira had helped the fauns escape as much as she had, and she had assumed he'd left on the ships with Sabina.

But the way Ava was asking her, she wasn't so sure anymore.

"He's gone," she said simply.

"You don't care at all about what he might be up to?" he asked.

"I'm not his keeper."

Ava gave her a cynical smirk. "Weren't you, though? Isn't that what Valefor tasked you with? Keeping Ira in line?"

"Mephis is the one who gave me the orders, and he's dead," Tris said coolly. "Ira is gone, and I am busy with a kingdom that is in total disarray, so no, I don't particularly care where he is."

"Do you know where he is or not, Ava?" Indy snapped. "Get to the point."

"Ira has aims to be King," Ava said.

"He wants to be King of Furorem?" Tris asked, assuming that he'd gone back to his homeland.

"No, not Furorem." Ava shook his head. "He wants to rule Desperationis."

"*What*?" Tris asked, and if it wasn't for Indy's arm around her, she would've gotten to her feet.

"He has been holed up with a team of sonneillons since the King died," Ava explained. "Wouldn't that be something? A peccati as the ruler of an entire kingdom? Not just playing consiliarius but making the actual decrees."

"Ira wants to be King of my kingdom?" she asked, incredulous. "He's a child, and he's been a peccati for... for minutes, practically."

"All of that is true," Ava said. "But don't you think it would be so much easier for him to gather enough sacrifices for the sangcoranimilia if he had an entire kingdom under his control?"

"Damn it." Tris cursed and ran a hand over her face. "I thought Dolorin was bad, but now I'll be expected to advise the Ira?"

"You need to direct him to our side," Ava said, as if that wouldn't already be obvious. "You have an opportunity. This could very well be the beginning of the end."

"Of Valefor, or of us?" she asked wryly.

"Either are an option, I suppose, although I certainly have a preference," Ava said. "Which is why I came here. I wanted to warn you about Ira so you'd be able to plan your next moves accordingly."

"Well, we'll come up with a plan," Indy said. "Thank you for the heads up."

Ava seemed taken aback by the abrupt change in tone, and honestly, Tris was, too. She wasn't thrilled about having Ava around, but he provided information. Besides that, with everything being as precarious as it was, she had to take help where she could find it, even if Ava was suspiciously helpful.

"Do you want to stay here tonight?" Tris asked Ava, and Indy bristled. "It's late, and we have a hammock you can take."

"That's very kind, but I already booked a room in town," Ava declined with exaggerated regret. "I wasn't sure the condition that your house would be in."

Tris stood up, so he followed suit. She walked him to the door, but Indy stayed seated at the table, watching them.

Ava stepped just outside the door and adjusted his expensive-looking jacket. He cast his eyes to the sky, and when he spoke, he kept his voice low enough that Indy couldn't hear from where he sat. "What do you suppose all this is?"

"What are you talking about?" Tris asked.

Ava looked at Tris, then passed her, to Indy. "The two of you. The Castimonia and the Luxuria. Peccati and virtus keep pairing off together. Doesn't that seem strange to you?"

It had occurred to Tris that it was strange that she and Industria cared so much for each other, especially so quickly, but she hadn't really thought of it as part of a pattern before.

"Have you ever met your opposite?" Tris asked, and the name of the Avaritia's virtu counterpart slipped her mind.

Ava averted his gaze, but not before she saw a flash of something in his eyes. "No. I haven't met very many virtus. I always thought I would hate to be around them..." He lifted his head and gave her a weak smile. "But it turns out that they're not all bad."

"Almost no one is," she agreed with a sigh.

The goodbyes seemed to have been said, but Ava continued to linger.

"Is there something else?" she asked.

"I..." He trailed off and chewed his lip.

"What?" she pressed.

His words were hardly even a whisper, so quiet they were nearly lost on the sea air, and his eyes were solemn when he looked at her. "I worry you don't trust me, and it's not that I blame you so much as I want you to heed my words. Be careful with him."

"Ava."

"Tris. There is a darkness in him. Maybe you can't see it, but I can," Ava persisted.

"There is darkness in us all," she replied quietly.

He exhaled deeply. "Maybe. But I need you in the days that are coming. Please. Just... *be careful*."

"You, too," Tris said. He nodded, then turned to start walking across the bridge. She stepped out and called after him. "How long are you staying in the city?"

He stopped long enough to answer, "I leave in the morning. I have elsewhere I need to be."

Tris waited another moment, leaning against the doorframe, and letting the sea spray cool her face. Before he made it to the mainland, she slipped back inside and locked the door behind her.

"What was all that about?" Indy got up and walked over to her.

She shrugged. "I know as much as you do."

200

"What did he say to you at the door?" he asked, and she couldn't tell if it was jealousy or fear that tightened his voice.

When Indy looked down at her, the gray steel of his eyes were the same ones she'd fallen in love with. In them, she saw love and strength, and if there was darkness, it was because the world around him had been so dark. Indy could not be expected to remain unchanged, not after all they had been through in recent weeks.

"He's worried and wants to make sure I'm on his side," she said, because she didn't want to worry Indy with Ava's perceptions, especially when she knew that they were wrong.

"Are you on his side?" Indy asked.

"Aren't *we*? I mean, I don't trust Ava. I don't really trust that many people outside of you. But we're working together, right? To keep Valefor away?"

"We are." He snaked an arm around her waist and pulled her closer to him. "And that's why I think you need to advise the council that Ira should be King."

Her smile instantly fell away. "That's preposterous, Indy. Everything I said to Ava was true. He's a petulant child!"

"How is that different than any other King you've known?" Indy countered.

"Every King I've known has been terrible. I was hoping for something better this time. And he is a direct servant to Valefor."

"So are you," he said gently, as if she needed reminding. "Ira knows you, and he trusts you already. Think about how much easier it will be to sway him away from dangerous rituals than it would be others.

201

He already helped the fauns. He's proven himself to be an ally."

"Except that he's apparently been hiding out in the city since Dolorin died, plotting to take over for him," Tris reasoned. "He hasn't spoken to me at all, so I can't be sure how much of an ally he is."

"No one on the council of nobles and sonneillons will ever be a true, complete ally for you," he persisted. "But we are working in a murky gray area. We have to use what we have."

She chewed the inside of her cheek and considered all that everyone had said tonight. "You think we should use Ira?"

He brushed back a lock of hair that fallen across her forehead, and he cradled her face in his hand as he said, "I think we need to do whatever we have to, if we want to protect those we care about."

She closed her eyes, then leaned into him and rested her head on his chest. His heart pounded slow and steady, and when he wrapped his arms around her, she'd honestly never felt safer in her entire life.

"I'm tired, and tomorrow is going to be a long, long, looooooong day," she murmured. "Can we just go to bed?"

He kissed the top of her head, and she felt his words rumbling in his chest before she heard them. "Of course. Anything you want, Tris."

CHAPTER THIRTY-FOUR

SOMEHOW, THERE WAS ALWAYS FAINT ETHEREAL music playing at Luminelle's, but Lily had never actually seen the performers. It seemed to emanate from everywhere, filling the space the same as the heady scent of lilacs.

Aeterna had brought Lily here, and he left her at the entrance, as he often did for her visits. Luminelle summoned Lily alone, but she couldn't travel to the other realms without an irin's help.

She climbed the steps, lifting the long hem of her pale blue gown, but she moved slowly today. The quick flight between realms had left her dizzy and weak, and she put her hand to her temple.

"Lily, is everything all right?" Luminelle asked in her lyrical voice, and she appeared in the vestibule.

"Yes, I am fine, honestly," Lily assured her. "I have just been a little tired lately, from all the business with the wedding and all the troubles that followed."

As she'd been talking, Luminelle's expression had shifted from concern to joy. Lily could only look up at her in bewilderment while her Mistress smiled.

"Lily, my sweet Castimonia," she cooed, and she put a hand on her belly. "You are with child."

"*What?*" Lily asked.

But the instant she heard the words, she knew they were true. A warm fluttering stirred in her abdomen, and she couldn't help but smile.

It was so soon, much sooner than she had planned to start a family with Maxon, but that didn't dampen the elation that she felt.

"I'm going to have a baby with Maxon." Then Lily looked to Luminelle. "But I've only just become the Castimonia. What will that mean for me? What will that mean for my child?"

"There will be nothing to worry about, and we have plenty of time to discuss it all." Luminelle looped an arm around Lily's shoulders and led her further into the airy palace, toward the sitting parlor.

"What did you want to discuss today?" Lily asked. "Since you invited me here?"

"I wanted to see how you were holding up with all the changes," Luminelle said. "You've been through a lot in a short amount of time, and I wanted to be sure you were happy and weren't getting overwhelmed."

"I think I am happy *and* also overwhelmed," she said honestly.

Luminelle laughed. "We'll go to my parlor and have some tea and see if we can help ease some of your stress."

They spent the afternoon talking and sipping tea, and to her surprise, much of the stress of the recent weeks had faded. Luminelle had even comforted Lily for her well-meaning blunder, rushing into an unfriendly kingdom without consulting anyone.

"I know you want to help, and there will be so much time for that in the future," Luminelle promised her as she squeezed her hand. "Right now, you need to focus on yourself and your baby. Everything else can wait."

"Even Valefor?" Lily asked in dismay.

Her Mistress gave her a thin smile. "What cannot wait is not your concern. I have many others serving me. We will handle Valefor."

"Does that mean you'll be returning to Cormundie?" Lily asked.

"Not yet," she replied, sounding almost sad, and she looked out to the flowers and plants that filled the sitting parlor. "But that too is for the best. If I cannot return, neither can Valefor. We are safe in our realms, and you will be safe in yours."

Shortly after that, Luminelle was called away for a meeting with several irins, and Aeterna returned Lily to her home.

Lily went up to her bedroom to change out of her travelling clothes, and she only just untied a solitary ribbon when she felt the warmth in her chest that she did whenever Maxon was near.

He came into their bedroom, smiling at her, and he greeted her the way he always did when they had been apart – he pulled her close and kissed her.

"How was your visit with Luminelle?" he asked, still holding her in his arms.

"It was really, really good. We talked, I drank some tea, and…" She could hardly hold back the smile as she looked up at him. "I have some news."

"Oh?" Instantly, his blue eyes darkened with worry. "What kind of news?"

"I'm pregnant, Maxon."

"What?" His face went lax in shock, and then a smile started to form at the corners of his mouth. "Really? How do you know?"

"Luminelle knew. She sensed it, and she told me."

"Lily, you're going to have a baby?" he asked, and he was nearly shouting in excitement. "We're going to have a baby?"

She nodded. "Yes. Are you happy?"

"I couldn't be happier. I never thought I'd find love, I never thought I'd be a father. Then I found you, and now we have a family."

She hadn't even really needed to ask. It was written all over his face. The pure joy and love left Maxon practically glowing.

They were both laughing and crying, and he held her close and covered her face in kisses.

CHAPTER THIRTY-FIVE

THE SONNEILLON BROUGHT INDY from Desperationis to the other realm and dropped him unceremoniously on the ground. It was a land made of rocks and brimstone, and he kicked up red dust as he fell.

"Thanks for the lift," Indy muttered, but the sonneillon was already gone. He had no idea what the sonneillons did around here, but since they always seemed to be in a hurry to do it, he had to assume it was something grotesque and terrible.

Valefor's palace was made of black marble with veins the color of blood swirling through. The palace was tall, empty, and dark, like walking into the vast darkness of space. Torches burned with amber flames, and Indy followed them down to the room in the center where Valefor seemed to spend his time.

He didn't know how he'd exactly define the room. Perhaps a chancery? Or maybe a library? It was another large box, with towering ceilings. The walls were shiny black marble, the ceilings and floor metallic and blood-red. There were two high back chairs, a small table, and a fireplace roaring, despite the heat. That was all for furniture.

Once Valefor had been reading a book when Indy arrived, another time he had just been sitting there and staring into the fire.

He tried not to think of what Valefor did in the room. He tried not to think of Valefor at all. But it was impossible to escape him.

When Indy finally entered the room, Valefor was standing at the fireplace. That was good, because it gave Indy a moment to steel himself before Valefor faced him.

Indy had been attracted to very few men in his life, but Valefor was undeniably handsome. He was something like perfection, and Indy hated thinking that, but it was true. The daemon was tall, even taller than him, and he had a penchant for being shirtless, showing off a physique that appeared like it had been chiseled from stone.

Even though the fire was behind him, Indy could somehow see the flames reflecting Valefor's pale eyes. His long hair was the color of burnt honey, and his voice was seductive like wine.

"You're looking well, Industria," Valefor greeted him with a smile.

"Can we skip the pleasantries?" Indy asked. "I promised to serve you, but we don't have to pretend to like one another."

"Why do you assume that I don't really like you?" Valefor asked, sounding puzzled.

Indy ran a hand through his hair and looked away from him. He was already sweating from the heat and nauseated from the travel, and he wasn't in the mood to play games with the daemon.

"I don't care if you like me," Indy said roughly. "I'm here to tell you that I've done as you asked."

"The Ira is King of Desperationis?"

"Yes."

"And Tris spoke up for him?" Valefor arched an eyebrow.

Indy nodded. "She did. The nobility weren't all on board with him, and she had to convince a few. But she did it."

"Excellent." Valefor clasped his hands together in front of him. "Now, we must begin to prepare for the sangcoranimilia."

Indy took a fortifying breath and tried to bite his tongue, but he couldn't hold it back. "I told you before, I don't think this is the right thing for you."

"And I've told you before that I don't give a damn what you think," Valefor seethed through his radiant smile.

"They won't let you do this!" Indy argued in exasperation. "I can't stop all of the virtus and half of the peccati! Not on my own. Not even if I wanted to."

The smile finally fell away from Valefor's face. He scowled and his eyes burned. "You *do* want to. You know the choice you've made. Tristitia lives because you do as I say, you want what I want, my will is your will." The daemon held up his hand like he meant to snap his fingers. "Otherwise I can take her away from you again like – "

"No," Indy said quickly. "Your will is my will. I'm doing all I can. I've done everything that you've asked so far. But I am telling you that I don't think you will be able to complete the sangcoranimilia. Not with the numbers you have."

"Well, you don't know all the numbers that I have," Valefor growled. "We will complete the ritual, and you will continue to do as I say. Are you ready for your instructions for your next part of the plan?"

Because there was no other answer he could give, he nodded and said, "Yes, Master."

MAPS

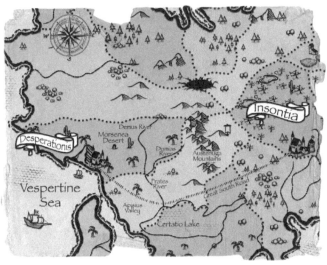

Seven
Fallen
Hearts

The saga
continues in
the next book.
Coming Late
2022

First Book Out Now

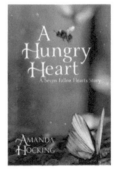

Short Story Coming Soon

www.HockingBooks.com

ABOUT THE AUTHOR

AMANDA HOCKING is the author of over twenty-five
novels, including the *New York Times* bestselling
Trylle Saga and the indie bestseller My Blood
Approves. Her love of pop culture and all things
paranormal influence her writing. She spends her time
in Minnesota, taking care of her menagerie of pets
and working on her next book.

To learn more, please visit www.HockingBooks.com

Made in United States
Troutdale, OR
01/21/2024